"You're extremely rude! I was actually beginning to like you.

"But I see now that you're exactly the same as you were when we met...."

"Do tell me." He sounded amused and not in the least repentant.

"Bad tempered and impatient and laughing at me." She drank the rest of her coffee and said in a small, polite voice, "Thank you for my lunch," and put out a hand to pick up her purse, but his own large hand came down, very gently, onto hers.

"I'm all those things, and more," he told her quietly, "but could you not like me a little despite them?"

She sat looking at his hand. It felt cool and strong, cherishing hers in its grasp—the hand of someone who would help her if ever she needed it. She said uncertainly, "I don't understand you, or know anything about you, but I do like you."

The hand tightened just a little. "Good," said the doctor.

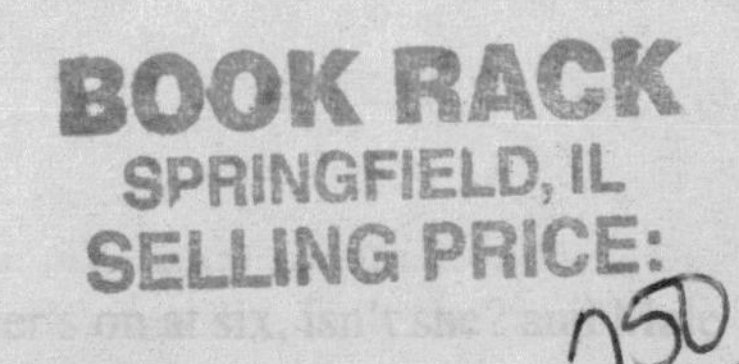

Romance readers around the world were sad to note the passing of **Betty Neels** in June 2001. Her career spanned thirty years, and she continued to write into her ninetieth year. To her millions of fans, Betty epitomized the romance writer, and yet she began writing almost by accident. She had retired from nursing, but her inquiring mind still sought stimulation. Her new career was born when she heard a lady in her local library bemoaning the lack of good romance novels. Betty's first book, *Sister Peters in Amsterdam,* was published in 1969, and she eventually completed 134 books. Her novels offer a reassuring warmth that was very much a part of her own personality. She was a wonderful writer, and she will be greatly missed. Her spirit and genuine talent will live on in all her stories.

THE BEST *of*

BETTY NEELS

The Edge of Winter

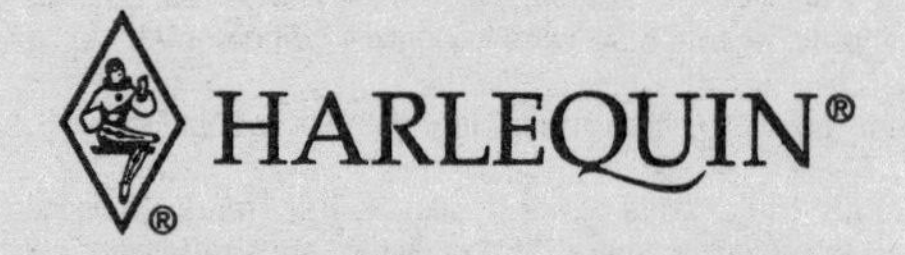

TORONTO • NEW YORK • LONDON
AMSTERDAM • PARIS • SYDNEY • HAMBURG
STOCKHOLM • ATHENS • TOKYO • MILAN • MADRID
PRAGUE • WARSAW • BUDAPEST • AUCKLAND

ISBN-13: 978-0-373-19961-7

THE EDGE OF WINTER

This edition published by arrangement with Harlequin Books S.A.

www.eHarlequin.com

Printed in U.S.A.

CHAPTER ONE

THE little town was small and snug, tucked in between the Cornish hills and cliffs, and the late afternoon sun shone on its slate roofs and brightened the whitewashed walls of the cottages clustered round its small harbour, although there was a chilly wind blowing in from the sea. It was not yet five o'clock, but the October afternoon was already drawing in, and the girl climbing the path from the harbour towards the car park at the side shivered a little as she paused to look back before she rounded the corner, to thread her way through the few cars there and then follow the cliff path.

It was a little late for a walk, she reflected, but she had been playing backgammon with her father all the afternoon, sitting in the lounge of the Lobster Pot Hotel, and she had stolen frequent glances out of the old-fashioned bow window overlooking the harbour and felt envy of the intrepid yachtsmen gowling briskly out to the open sea. It would have been nice to have gone sailing, but although several of the younger men staying in the little town had scraped the beginnings of an acquaintance with her, it had come to nothing; her father and aunt had absorbed all her leisure, and quite unwittingly; they were darlings and she loved them devotedly, but they tended to forget that she was all of twenty-five with a responsible job, a life of her own, and well able to take care of herself.

She turned her back on the harbour, left the car park behind and took the path along the cliff top. Round the next great headland of grey rock was Falmouth, but it might have been a hundred miles away, for there was nothing to see but the rough grass around her and the sea below. She stopped again to watch the gulls wheeling in from the sea; the wind was freshening, but despite this there were still two or three sailing boats out to sea and she sat down for a moment on a tussock of coarse grass the better to watch them, pulling the high neck of her sweater closer and retying her long honey-coloured hair. She was a pretty girl, with large dark blue eyes fringed with honey-coloured lashes which she didn't darken and a straight little nose above a generous mouth; her long legs were encased in old slacks and when she stood up she showed herself to be a little above middle height and slim without being skinny.

The path was a narrow one, sometimes running close to the cliff edge so that she had a clear view of the sea surging amongst the rocks below, sometimes turning inland between trees and shrubs. She walked briskly, her thoughts busy. Tomorrow she would be leaving Cornwall and returning to London; to St Katherine's, where she was the Accident Room Sister, and in a way, she reflected, she wouldn't mind going back. She loved her father and Aunt Martha dearly, but they were elderly now, content to sit with a book or play cards and take a daily walk along the harbour, activities which weren't enough for her own youthful energy. But the week of doing almost nothing had done her good; she felt rested and relaxed, ready to tackle a hard day's work, and besides, there was another week's holiday to look forward to—just before Christmas, when she would go home to the pleasant little house in its small, well kept garden, tucked tidily into one of the narrow side streets of the Somerset village where she had been born and brought up. It was delightful once the summer tourists had gone, with its wide main street and Dunster Castle towering over it, and if she felt like it, she could walk down to the water to catch a glimpse of Wales on the other side of it, and if that wasn't enough, there was always Minehead a mile or so away.

The path had found its way back to the edge of the cliff once more and she slowed her pace to watch the clouds bunched angrily on the horizon. It would rain, but not yet. She had time to walk back to the hotel without fear of getting wet, and the faint sea mist beginning to creep up didn't worry her either; she had walked the path almost daily and knew it well enough.

She was on the point of turning back when her eye caught something moving far below her—something white. There was someone there, waving, and leaning precariously over the cliff face, she could hear a faint treble shout. She looked carefully round her; there was no boat within miles and certainly no other human being, and right before was an apology of a path, trickling out of sight down the rough cliff face. Someone had apparently gone down that way and was unable to get back. She could, of course, go back to the town and get help, but that would take too long; it would be dark by then and almost certainly raining. Whoever it was down there was unable to walk or climb and they would get soaked and cold. If she went down now, she and the unfortunate below would be back on the cliff top within fifteen minutes or so, and if they were injured and couldn't climb—well, all the more reason for her to go down and see what could be done.

The path was steep but perfectly safe, and she didn't find it too difficult; heights didn't bother her and she was surefooted enough. She was halfway down when she saw that it was a child on the little patch of sand between the sharp spines of rock, and she quickened her pace, for the child wasn't moving.

It was a girl, a little girl of eight or so, with a small face puffed and red with tears and one leg bent awkwardly beneath her. She was wearing shorts and it was her T-shirt which she had been waving.

She said at once in a hoarse little voice: 'I thought no one would ever come—what's your name?'

'Araminta Shaw—what's yours?' Araminta recognised that an exchange of names spelled security for the child, and smiled cheerfully at her.

'I'm Mary Rose Jenkins and I've hurt my leg—I fell…' She burst into tears, and Araminta sat down beside her and hugged her close and let her cry. Presently she wailed: 'I can't move it—I tried, but it hurts. What shall we do?' She looked round with an anxious face. 'It's getting dark.'

'Not yet, it's not,' said Araminta, and eyed the telltale bump, already discoloured, just above the child's thin ankle. A Pott's fracture, and how on earth was she going to find anything to splint it, and even if she found it, how were they going to get up the cliff again? Piggyback, if the child could bear the pain and she herself could manage the path with the uncertain weight of the child on her shoulders; she would tackle that problem when she came to it. Now she said cheerfully: 'Let's put that shirt back on, and then I'm going to do something about that leg of yours. You see, we must get it straight, poppet, before we climb back up that cliff path. I shall hurt you, I'm afraid, but you're a brave girl, aren't you?'

She dropped a kiss on the tangled brown hair, slid the shirt back on and studied their surroundings; surely there would be some wood lying around; an old box, a broken spar, even some cardboard. There was always flotsam and jetsam on the sea shore. 'Look, Mary Rose,' she explained, 'I want to find a piece of wood to tie to your leg—it won't hurt nearly as much then. Will you be OK while I look round? I won't go far.'

There was nothing, absolutely nothing at all. She went back to where the child waited so patiently and sat down beside her and took off the knee socks she was wearing under her slacks; they were by no means ideal, but she could tie the little girl's legs together, using the sound leg as a splint. She told Mary Rose what she was going to do, begged her to keep as still as she could, and bent to her task. In hospital, she reflected, with everything to hand, the fracture could have been reduced and the leg put in plaster with the child happily unconscious under anaesthetic; now all she dared to do was to lift the little broken leg gently until it was beside its fellow and tie her socks above and below the fracture. Mary Rose screamed all the while she was doing it, but she had to shut her ears to that; all she could do when she had finished was to hold the child close and soothe her, and presently, as the pain dulled a little, Mary Rose dozed off.

Araminta sat awkwardly, the child's small body pressed close to hers, while she debated what to do next. To go up the cliff path was going to be so difficult that it would be almost impossible; but to stay there all night was impossible too, an opinion borne out by the first few drops of rain. They became a downpour within minutes, and the wind, still freshening, sent scuds of spray on to the small stretch of sand. Really, thought Araminta, it couldn't be worse. There was no shelter, and Mary Rose had wakened and was voicing her displeasure in no uncertain manner. Araminta, who didn't quail easily, quailed now. 'This,' she declared strongly, 'is the utter end!'

Only it wasn't; a yacht was coming round the next headland, still some way off, but at least sailing in their direction. She waved, wishing she had something colourful which the people on board might see more easily in the deepening gloom, told Mary Rose the good news, laid her down carefully and then went right to the water's edge and waved again. The yacht turned a little away from them, out to sea, giving the rocky coast a wide berth; probably those on board hadn't even seen her. But she went on waving even though her arms ached; she shouted too, quite uselessly, but it made her feel better. When the yacht turned again, inland this time, she hardly dared to hope that she had been seen. She watched anxiously to see what would happen next and shouted with delight when its slender nose was pointed towards land. She waved again and then went to reassure Mary Rose, who had rolled over on to her bad leg and was screaming with pain. Araminta bent over the child, doing the best she could, and when she straightened, it was to see a rubber dinghy nosing its way slowly through the treacherous water between the outcrops of rock. She ran down to the water again, peering through the driving rain, and splashed into the surf, already so wet that she hardly noticed the water round her ankles.

'Oh, what a blessing!' she cried happily. 'I've never been so glad to see anyone in my life—I thought we'd be stuck here…'

The occupant of the dinghy cut its motor, pulled it half out of the water and stood up. He was a big, heavily built man and very tall, with dark hair greying at the temples; his hawklike good looks wore a look of extreme ill-humour as he stood looking down at her. He was just as wet as she was, his thick sweater heavy with rain and sea water, his slacks sopping. He said harshly: 'You silly little fool—don't you know that these cliffs are dangerous?' He caught sight of Mary Rose. 'And what's that?'

Araminta eyed him with disfavour; he might have come to their rescue, but he didn't need to be quite so nasty about it. She said snappily:

'That is a little girl—she's broken her leg, I certainly shouldn't have waved to you otherwise; I'm perfectly capable of climbing the cliff path.'

He smiled nastily. 'My dear good woman, I'm not in the least interested in your climbing prowess. How do you know the child's leg is broken?' He was by Mary Rose's side now, sitting on his heels, not touching anything, just looking. 'A Pott's,' he murmured, and Araminta said in a surprised voice: 'Yes, it is—how did you know?'

'I'm a doctor,' he answered her blandly as he gently undid the socks, 'and how did you know?'

'I'm a nurse.'

'You surprise me.' He ignored her gasp of annoyance, and bent to see the extent of the damage. He retied the socks presently, saying coolly: 'Well, at least you had the sense to leave it alone. I'll get her on board and put in at Mousehole. She can go to Falmouth by ambulance.'

'Can't you sail back to Falmouth?' Araminta wanted to know. 'It's quite close…' He gave her a withering look. 'The wind,' he explained with a frosty patience which set her teeth on edge. 'We should have to sail into it and it would take twice as long.' He bent over the child again and his dark face was lighted by a smile now. 'We're all going back home in my boat,' he told her. 'Once we are there we'll get that leg seen to.' He touched Mary Rose's brown hair with a gentle finger. 'What a brave little girl you are!' He stood up and looked out to sea to where the yacht was anchored. 'Get into the dinghy,' he ordered Araminta, 'and sit down. I'll put the child in your lap.'

She did as she was told, seething silently. Now was hardly the time to tell someone—someone who was rescuing them from an unpleasant situation—that she considered him to be the rudest man she had ever encountered. She cuddled the little girl close during the short journey, and only when they reached the yacht did she wonder how on earth they were to get on board.

She need not have worried; there was someone waiting for them, a grey-haired, thick-set elderly man with powerful arms, who reached over the boat's side and lifted Mary Rose as though she had been a feather and disappeared below with her. Araminta watched the yacht dancing in the choppy sea and wondered what she was supposed to do. 'Hold the rail,' her companion advised her, 'and pull yourself aboard—it's quite easy. Wait until I say so.'

It didn't look in the least easy, but she was beyond

worrying about it; when he said 'Right,' she pulled herself up and helped by an unexpected boost from behind, landed untidily on the yacht's deck. It didn't help at all to see the man spring lightly on deck beside her without any effort at all and proceed to tie up the dinghy. 'Go below,' he said over his shoulder. And she went.

It was warm and snug in the cabin. Mary Rose was on a padded couch along one wall and the elderly man was pouring tea into four mugs. He looked up as their rescuer joined them and spoke in a language Araminta couldn't understand, and when he nodded, fetched a bottle and poured some of its contents into the mugs. 'Brandy,' said the dark man, 'and get those wet clothes off—and the child's, too.' He went to a locker and pulled out a couple of sweaters and some blankets.

'Use these.'

Araminta didn't say anything; not because she could think of nothing to say; there was a great deal she was storing up for a more suitable occasion—besides, her teeth were chattering too hard to make speech effective. She gave Mary Rose some of the hot tea and drank her own. The brandy sent a warm glow through her and she was on the point of remonstrating with their unwilling host when he urged the child to drink the rest of her tea, but he forestalled her with a quiet: 'Yes, I know what you're about to say, but we have an hour's sailing before us and the sea's choppy—she needs to sleep.'

He swallowed his own tea, spoke to the older man and went on deck, to be followed at once by his companion.

Araminta began to undress Mary Rose—luckily there was almost nothing to take off; the sweater was far too large, but it was warm and enveloped the child completely. She wrapped a blanket round her and saw with relief that she was already half asleep.

It didn't take her more than a moment to tear off her own sweater and put on the one she had been given. She was forced to turn up its sleeves to half their length, and it was so long that she debated whether to take off her slacks as well, but she decided against that; she wouldn't look dignified, and she wanted to be that at all costs. She settled for damp slacks and her dignity, plaited her damp hair and longed for a mirror. The yacht was moving now, and just as its owner had said, the sea was choppy; she supposed it was the brandy which made her feel so unconcerned about it.

Mary Rose was deeply asleep now and likely to remain so, what with fright and pain and brandy. Araminta pulled up a stool and sat by the couch, one arm over the child, and looked about her. She knew very little about yachts, but this one struck her as extremely comfortable; its furnishings were simple, but there was no lack of comfort. She fell to wondering who the owner might be and why he had spoken in a foreign tongue to the other man. She frowned a little; he had spoken fluent English to her, but now that she thought about it, there had been the faintest accent. The object of her thoughts came back at that moment, walking through the cabin without a word, to enter a cubby-hole at its end which presumably held radio equipment, for she could hear his voice speaking to someone, but when he came back it was obvious to her from his aloof expression that he had no intention of telling her anything. He said nothing, only opened a cupboard in the wall, took out a packet of sandwiches and laid them on the table beside her.

Araminta ate two of them, for she was peckish. The

walk had sharpened her appetite and then there had been the climb down the cliffs and some considerable time waiting beside the child. The sandwiches were excellent—smoked salmon and very fresh brown bread; she eyed the rest of them hungrily as she wrapped them up again, but Mary Rose might wake and feel hungry too. But she didn't; not once during the rest of the rather unpleasant hour did she stir, and a good thing too, thought Araminta, for the sea was now quite rough and the wind had veered, slowing their progress. The elderly man had come below briefly to give her another mug of coffee and ask her, in his peculiar English, if she needed anything and was the little girl all right. She accepted the coffee gratefully, not moving from her stool, and wondered as she drank it if anyone had missed the child yet. Surely by now—she glanced at the clock and saw to her astonishment that it was almost half past eight; they must have been on the beach much longer than she had thought. Her father and Aunt Martha would certainly be wondering where she was, and Mary Rose's parents would be frantic… Her thoughts were interrupted once more by the dark man, who stayed just long enough to tell her that they would be entering the harbour within the next few minutes. He disappeared as quickly as he had come.

She knew almost nothing about sailing, but it seemed to her that the yacht was berthed very smoothly and in a few minutes both men came into the cabin; when the boat's owner bent to pick the little girl up, Araminta observed urgently: 'She's very sound asleep. She's all right, isn't she?'

His severe expression softened into a brief smile. 'She's a very little girl and she's had a lot of brandy.'

There was nothing she could answer to that; she picked up their damp clothes and followed him up on deck. It was raining still and very dark, and there was no sign of the wind easing. There were a few lights here and there, shining through the curtain of rain, but no one about. The three of them made their way silently down the small harbour's arm and on to the quayside, the little girl cradled in the dark man's arms, Araminta close at his heels and behind her the elderly man, walking stolidly into the rain.

Araminta skipped a step or two and caught up with the leader of the party. 'Where are we going?'

'A pub—somewhere where there are people who will know whose child this is and where we can telephone.'

'There's the Lobster Pot just along here.' She waved into the dimly lighted narrow street ahead of them, which ran round the harbour. 'They're...'

'I know—I've been here before.'

'How rude,' said Araminta severely, and went past him to open the hotel door. It was in the side wall of the hotel and led straight into the downstairs bar. There were quite a number of people in it, among them her father and aunt, in deep discussion with the hotel's owner, but they paused in mid-sentence when they saw her and her companions, and Aunt Martha, a formidable-looking lady with severe features and a well-disciplined hair style, made her way briskly through the throng around her and demanded briskly: 'Araminta, where have you been? We've been very worried—and who are these people?'

Her sharp eyes took in the child in the man's arms and his companion and then returned to her bedraggled niece.

'Sorry you were worried, Aunt,' said Araminta, knowing that under the rather fierce exterior was a very nice old lady who loved her. 'I found this little girl, and these gentlemen very kindly picked us up in their yacht and brought us back. The child's leg is broken and this gentleman is a doctor, so if…' she paused and looked at him, standing silently beside her. 'If you would say what you want us to do?' she asked him. 'A room with a firm table—something I can use for splints, and someone to telephone for an ambulance to take the child to hospital and to discover to whom she belongs.'

It was like being back at St Katherine's, carrying out a consultant's orders without waste of time. 'There's an office behind the reception desk, I'm sure the owner…' She was already there, asking for its use and if someone would see about the ambulance. 'Two sticks,' she reminded herself aloud and heard the man chuckle; worse, he followed it with a: 'You've more sense than I imagined.' He spoke in a faintly mocking voice which made her grit her splendid teeth. But it was no time to consider her own feelings, so she pushed the table into a better position and went to fetch the variety of sticks offered as well as a splendid collection of scarves, ties and napkins to tie them with. She chose the most suitable of them, smiled briefly at her father, standing quietly in a corner, and went back to where Mary Rose, still mercifully tipsy, lay.

She admitted to herself later that the child's bony little leg had been expertly splinted, the ends of the bone brought into alignment before the splints were put on; probably they were in as good a position as they needed to be before the plaster was applied. It was a pity she would never know that; Mary Rose had been whisked off to Falmouth in the ambulance and the dark man had gone with her, while his companion had gone back to the yacht. Both men had said goodbye to her, the elder with grave courtesy, the younger with a curt brevity which allowed her to see that he couldn't care less if he never saw her again.

She went to bed much later, having repeated her story a great many times for the benefit of her father and aunt, the owner of the hotel and most of the guests staying at the hotel. The police had come too, bringing with them a distraught young woman who had slipped out to the shops, thinking it was safe to leave her small daughter alone for a little while. Araminta answered the policeman's questions, accepted the woman's thanks awkwardly and asked if the child was safely in hospital. The police sergeant said that yes, she was, with the leg nicely plastered, and that the gentleman who had been such a help us there too. Possibly, he added, Araminta herself would see him on the following day, for he would be returning to his yacht.

But in the morning there was no sign of him, although the yacht was still in the harbour. Araminta, put out for no good reason, dressed in her well-cut tweed suit, put her shining hair up in a neat coil on the top of her pretty head, got into her elderly Mini and began the drive back to London. Her father and aunt saw her off. Her father, as usual, had very little to say beyond wishing her a good journey and not too much work. It was Aunt Martha who said in her measured tones:

'That was an interesting man who brought you back yesterday. A pity you won't see him again, my dear.'

Araminta put a stylishly shod foot down on the accelerator. 'He was the rudest man I've ever met,' she pronounced coldly. 'The only pity is that I shan't see him to tell him so.'

CHAPTER TWO

ST KATHERINE'S was one of the older hospitals, maintaining its proud reputation despite its out-of-date wards, its endless corridors and numerous, quite unnecessary flights of stairs. It looked particularly depressing and down-at-heel as Araminta parked the Mini in the shed reserved for the nursing staff and walked across the wide forecourt and in through the hospital's forbidding entrance. She had driven the two hundred and seventy-odd miles with only the shortest of breaks and it had taken her eight hours; she was tired and hungry and anxious to get to her small basement flat not five minutes' walk away from the hospital, but first she had to let Pamela Carr, the relief Sister who had been doing her duties for her, know that she was back, so that she wouldn't need to come on duty in the morning. She found her in the Accident Room, and for once there was a mere handful of patients there, and none of those in dire need. Sylvia Dawes was there too, sitting in the office, frowning over the pile of forms on the desk. She was a small, neat girl, Junior Sister on the department and a great friend of Araminta. She looked up as she went in and said in a relieved voice: 'Oh, good, you're back—now I can leave these wretched things for you. Did you have a good time?'

Araminta perched on the edge of the desk, 'Lovely. Quiet—rotten weather most of the time, though, but a smashing hotel; oak beams and comfy chairs and gorgeous food.'

'No men?'

She shook her head. 'Middle-aged, and one or two sailing enthusiasts.'

'Did you go sailing, then?'

'No—yes—well, I did, just once.'

'Was it fun?'

Araminta allowed her thoughts to dwell on the ill-tempered giant who had rescued her and Mary Rose. 'No, not really,' she admitted, and felt regret that it hadn't been. 'Anything happen while I was away?'

'The usual,' Sylvia told her, and Araminta nodded her head. 'The usual' covered a multitude of things: road accidents, small children who had fallen into the washing machine, old ladies with fractured thighs, old men dying for lack of warmth or good food, housewives who had fallen off chairs while hanging the curtains, youths with broken noses and badly cut up faces, coronaries, and distraught men and women of all ages who had taken an overdose. She got off the desk, said: 'Oh, well—back to work tomorrow. Pam's off in the morning, isn't she? Are we on together at eight o'clock?'

Sylvia nodded. 'I'm off at one o'clock and then two days off—you've got Staff Nurse Getty, though, and that nice Mrs Pink as well as two students.'

Araminta nodded in her turn. 'I'm going home now—see you in the morning.' She said goodnight and went back to the Mini and drove herself back into the street, to turn into a narrow, dark thoroughfare not a stone's throw away. It was lined with grim Victorian houses, all exactly alike and all long since turned into flats. She stopped half way down the terrace, opened the squeaky area gate and descended the steps to the neatly painted door of her flat, and went inside. There was the tiniest of lobbies leading to a quite large sitting room where she cast down her handbag, wound the clock, switched on the radio and then went back to the car for her luggage before driving a few yards down the road where she had a lock up garage. The little car safely stowed, she went back to the flat, shut the door on the dark evening and went along to the minute kitchen to put on the kettle.

The little place looked pleasant enough with the lamps switched on and the gas fire burning; she went to the bedroom next and unpacked her case, then made tea and sat down to drink it, casting a housewifely eye round her as she did so. The place needed a good dust, otherwise it was as clean and tidy as she had left it; its cheerful red carpet brushed, the colourful cushions nicely plumped up, the small round table where she had her meals shining with polish. It was a very small flat and rather dark on account of it being almost a basement, but Araminta counted herself lucky to have a home of her own, and so close to her work, too.

She poured herself a second cup and looked through her post; the electricity bill, a leaflet asking her if she had any old iron or scrap metal, and a letter or two from friends who had married and gone to live in other parts of the country. She read them all in turn and poured more tea. 'What I would really like,' she told herself out loud, 'would be a huge box of wildly expensive flowers and a note begging me to spend the evening at one of those places where the women wear real diamonds and there's a champagne bucket on very table.' She kicked off her shoes for greater comfort. 'I should have to wear that pink dress,' she mused, absorbed in her absurd daydream, 'and I'd be fetched by someone in a Rolls—the best there is—driven by…' She stopped, because the dark, bad-tempered man in the yacht had suddenly popped into her head, so clearly that there was no question of anyone else taking his place.

'Fool,' said Araminta cheerfully, and took the tray out to the kitchen.

The morning began badly with a severely burned toddler being brought in by a terrified mother. Araminta, her honey-coloured hair crowned by a frilled cap, her slim person very neat in its navy blue uniform and white apron, sent an urgent message to James Hickory, the Casualty Officer, to leave his breakfast and come at once, and began the difficult task of saving the child's life; putting up a plasma drip, assembling the equipment they would need, preparing the pain-killing drug the small screaming creature needed so urgently. It was an hour or more before Mr Hickory, the redoubtable Mrs Pink and Araminta had done everything necessary; the small, unconscious form was wheeled away to the ICU at last, and she was able to turn her attention to the less serious cases which had come in and which Staff Nurse Getty was dealing with.

The morning followed its usual pattern after that, with a steady stream of patients arriving, being treated, and dispatched, either home again or to the appropriate ward, and because there was a sudden rush at midday,

Araminta didn't go to the dining room for her dinner, but gobbled a sandwich, washed down with a pot of tea, in her office. She didn't mind much; she was off duty at five o'clock; she would cook herself a meal when she got home, go to bed early and read. Viewed from the peak hour of a busy day, the prospect was delightful.

She managed to get over to the Nurses' Home for tea; the Sisters had a sitting room there, and it had long been the custom for them to foregather at four o'clock, that was if they could spare the time. There had been a break in the steady stream of patients coming into the Accident Room, and Araminta, leaving Mrs Pink—a trained nurse of wide experience—in charge, felt justified in taking her tea break.

There was quite a crowd in the sitting room, bunched round the electric fire while Sister Bates, by virtue of her seniority both in service and in years, poured out. Araminta squeezed in between a striking redhead of fragile appearance, who ruled Men's Medical with an iron hand, and a small, mousey girl who looked as though she couldn't say bo to a goose, but who nevertheless held down the exacting job of ENT Theatre Sister. They both said: 'Hi—how's work after the Cornish fleshpots?'

'Foul,' declared Araminta succinctly. 'That trachie we sent you—how's it going?' she asked the mousey girl, and the three of them talked shop for a few minutes while they drank their tea and ate toast and the remains of someone's birthday cake. 'Going out this evening?' asked Debby, the redhead.

Araminta shook her head. 'Supper round the fire, bed and a book.'

'And that will be the last time for weeks,' observed

Sister Bates, who had been eavesdropping quite shamelessly. 'Who's the current admirer?'

Araminta grinned up at her from her place on the floor. 'Batesy dear, I haven't got one…'

Sister Bates frowned with mock severity. 'You've got dozens—well, all the unattached housemen for a start. I've never met such a girl!' But her blue eyes twinkled as she spoke. Araminta was so very pretty and nice with it; she never lacked for invitations although everyone knew that she never angled for them, they just dropped into her lap and she accepted them, whether they were rather grand seats at the theatre or a quick egg and chips at the little café round the corner, and not even her worst enemy—and she had none, anyway—could accuse her of going out of her way to encourage any of the men who asked her out, and she made no bones about putting them in their place if she found it necessary. Sister Bates thought of her as an old-fashioned girl, an opinion which might have annoyed Araminta if she had known about it. She had a great many friends and liked them all, men and women alike. That she got on well with men was a fact which didn't interest her greatly; one day she would meet a man she would love and, she hoped, marry, but until then she was just a pleasant girl to take out and remarkably unspoilt.

But for the next few evenings she stayed in her little flat, catching up on her letter writing, re-covering the cushions in the sitting room and painting the tiny kitchen. She made such a good job of this that she decided to paint the sitting room too, a task she began a few days later, for she had her two days off; ample time in which to finish the job. She came off duty full of enthusiasm for the idea, had a hurried meal, got into paint-smeared sweater and slacks, piled her bits and pieces of furniture into the centre of the room and started. She had just finished the door and was about to start on the wainscoting when someone banged the front door knocker and she put down her brush with a tut of impatience. It wasn't late, barely seven o'clock, but already dark, and she had no idea who it might be—true, James Hickory had wanted to take her to the cinema, but she had refused him firmly, and any of the other Sisters would have called through the letterbox. She got to her unwilling feet and opened the door, sliding the chain across as she did so. The dark giant who had rescued them from the beach was standing on the steps outside and she stood staring at him, round-eyed, for a few moments before exclaiming: 'Well, I never—however did you know that I live here?'

His eyes dropped to the chain and he smiled faintly. 'Your aunt gave me your address.'

'Aunt Martha? Why on earth should she do that?'

'I asked her for it. I thought you might like to hear about Mary Rose.'

'Oh, that's why you came. Come in.' Araminta slid back the chain and allowed him to enter. 'I'm painting my sitting room, but do sit down for a minute—I'll make some coffee.' She led the way into the muddle. 'There's a chair if you don't mind turning it right side up—I'll go...'

He filled the little room, she began to edge past him, conscious that she was glad to see him even though she didn't like him at all, and then came to a halt when he said: 'Is that the kitchen through there? Suppose I make the coffee and you can go on painting. May I take off my coat?'

'Yes, of course.' She hoped she didn't sound ungracious, but really, he had a nerve, though perhaps he only wanted to be kind. She took a quick look at his face and decided that he looked more like a robber baron than a do-gooder. She picked up the brush once more and got down on to her knees, feeling that she had rather lost her grip on the situation. 'I don't know your name,' she called through the open door, and then as he showed himself in the open doorway, 'Mind that paint, I've just done it.'

'Van Sibbelt—Crispin,' he told her, and disappeared to turn off the kettle. He was back again presently with their coffee mugs on a tray. He handed her one, offered the sugar and sat down on the wooden box she had been standing on to reach the top of the door.

'About Mary Rose,' he observed easily, 'she's doing very well, clumping round in a leg plaster.' He saw her look of enquiry and added placidly: 'I telephoned to find out.'

'I'm glad she's OK' Araminta felt a little out of her depth. 'It was very nice of you to let me know.' She sipped her coffee. 'You live in London?'

'No.'

A not very satisfactory answer, but she tried again. 'You're not English, are you? Your name—isn't it Dutch?'

'Yes.'

She put down her mug with something of a thump. 'Look, I'm not being curious—just making polite conversation. In fact,' she added with some asperity, 'I've every right to be curious, for I can't think why you should go to the trouble of coming here. If my aunt gave you my address you could just have well sent a postcard about Mary Rose.'

He regarded her in silence, his face a little austere, then

just as she was beginning to feel uncomfortable, he said: 'I wanted to see you again.'

At the very last second she thought better of asking him why, but instead she asked him, very nicely, if he would go. 'Such a pity that you should call at an awkward time, but you can see that I'm at sixes and sevens with this painting—you don't mind, do you? Do finish your coffee first, though.'

He looked as though he was going to laugh, but instead he said gravely, 'I see how busy you are. If you have a second brush I will do those bookshelves for you—half an hour's work at the most—it would help you a good deal.'

She got to her feet, which was a mistake, because he stood up too, towering over her, making her feel very small and at a disadvantage. All the same, she said a little coldly: 'It's most kind of you to offer, but I can manage all the same, thanks.'

'The brush-off,' he murmured, and grinned disarmingly, so that instead of looking like a well-dressed man of forty or so, he was a boy enjoying a splendid joke with himself.

'Men,' thought Araminta, crossly, watching him put on his coat again. Here he was, walking in and out of her life just as the fancy took him. She wished him goodbye in an austere voice and closed the door firmly on his broad back.

She went on painting until very late; the book-shelves proved awkward to do and she had to stand on the box again. The second time she fell off she was unable to refrain from wishing that she had accepted Dr van Sibbelt's kind offer.

She finished towards evening the next day and that

left her with a whole day more in which to plant spring bulbs in the troughs and pots which lined the tiny paved area outside her front door. She lingered over the task, looking up and down the street from time to time—perhaps Doctor van Sibbelt was still in London, and despite his cool reception, would come again to see her. He didn't; she went indoors, washed her hair, did her nails and watched a boring programme on TV before going to bed early.

She had been on duty barely an hour the next morning when they were all startled by an explosion, its repercussions rumbling on and on, so that even the solidly built Accident Room shook a little.

'A bomb,' said Araminta, busy at her desk, and left her papers to hurry into the department. It wasn't the first time; they all knew what to do, they were ready by the time James Hickory reached them with the news that they would be receiving the casualties. Such patients as there were were moved to one end of the receiving area with a borrowed houseman to look after them. Araminta sent a student nurse to look after him and went to answer the telephone. There would be twenty odd casualties, said an urgent voice, mostly glass wounds, but there were still some people trapped.

She relayed the information to James, telephoned for another houseman and went to cast a trained eye over the preparations. There would be more nurses coming within a few minutes and probably Debby, who wasn't on duty, but would return if she were near enough. Araminta took off her cuffs, rolled up her sleeves and went to meet the first ambulance, its sing-song wail reaching a crescendo as it stopped before the open doors.

There were two stretcher cases; the other two, both

men, were walking, helped by the ambulance men. They were covered in dust and nasty little cuts from flying glass and wore the look of men who had been severely shocked. Araminta consigned them to Mrs Pink and turned her attention to the stretcher cases. They were both unconscious, badly cut about the head and face, and one of them had an arm in a rough sling. She set to work on them, with calm speed, following James' careful instructions; they had barely dealt with them and sent them up to waiting theatre, before the second ambulance arrived.

After that, time didn't matter. They kept steadily on, coping with the stream of patients, seeing that the very ill ones had priority, and Araminta had the added task of seeing that her team of nurses, now swollen by extra help sent from the wards, were deployed to their best advantage. It was fortunate that a number of the victims were only slightly injured, so that after having cuts stitched, bruises treated and a hot drink, they were able to be sent to their homes. But that still left a hard core of badly injured, and some of them she could see wouldn't be fit to be moved for a little while yet; not only were they badly injured, they were filthy dirty, with hair full of glass splinters and torn clothes which had to be carefully cut away so that they might be examined for the minute but dangerous wounds made by metal splinters and slivers of glass and wood. She was cutting away the hair from a scalp wound when another ambulance arrived and within seconds the ambulance men were coming through the door with the stretcher between them, not waiting for the porters' help. Araminta knew both the men well; solid, reliable, not easily put out, but they looked worried enough now.

She handed her scissors to the student nurse who was helping her and hurried across the littered department, sweeping a trolley along with her.

'I take it it's urgent, George?' She eyed the grey face above the blanket.

'Just got 'im out, they 'ave, Sister—lorst a leg. There'll be a copper along with details—'e's in a bad way.'

She looked around her. Everyone was busy; a houseman was disappearing through a door carrying a child, the nurses were stretched to their limit, James and the house physician who had come to give a hand were bending over an elderly woman, who, not seriously hurt when she was admitted, had collapsed with a coronary. Someone would have to come. The ambulance men slid the stretcher on to the trolley and swung it into an empty bay and she lifted the blanket.

The patient, if he were to be saved, would need a blood transfusion before anything else. Araminta bade the ambulance men goodbye and picked up one of the small glass tubes lying ready on the dressing trolley; at least she could get a specimen of blood while she waited for a doctor. She was putting the cork back in when she was addressed from behind.

It was the senior consultant surgeon, Sir Donald Short.

'Ah, Sister, you appear to need help.' She had never been so thankful to hear his rather gruff voice. 'Perhaps we could give a hand.' He had come round the foot of the trolley and was already taking off his jacket. 'I see you have taken some blood—good. Run along to the Path Lab and get it cross-matched—and look sharp about it.' He lifted the blanket in his turn. 'We must do what we can for this poor fellow.'

Araminta didn't stop to speak. There was no need to

detail the man's injuries; she turned round to do as she had been told and found her way blocked by Sir Donald's companion—Doctor van Sibbelt, no less. The interesting and strangely disturbing fact registered itself upon her busy mind to be dismissed immediately; there were other, more important matters on hand.

By the time she got back with the two vacoliters of blood, the two men were hard at work with artery forceps, tying off carefully as they went. Sir Donald barely glanced at her, and Doctor van Sibbelt didn't look up at all.

'Get that up, Sister,' the consultant commanded. 'Crispin, see if you can find a vein in that arm—we'll run in the first liter as fast as we can and follow it with the second before we take him to theatre.' He paused for only a moment. 'Finished, Sister? Get hold of main theatre and tell them I want it ready in five minutes.'

He watched his companion slide the canulla into a limp vein. 'Crispin, will you give the anaesthetic? It'll relieve the pressure on the other theatres.' He added sharply: 'We need more blood, Sister.'

'It's on its way, sir,' Araminta was unflurried, 'and I'll see that it goes to theatre.'

'Good girl—let me have a pad here, then. Poor devil!'

Araminta took a blood pressure which only just registered. The face on the pillow was grey with shock; it could have belonged to an old man, although it was a mere lad lying there. She pitied him with all her warm heart but there was no time for pity; efficiency and gentleness and speed—above all, speed, came first. She could pity him later.

She sped away to telephone theatre, and saw as she went that the place was at last almost empty—there were still three or four patients waiting to be warded, and a handful of slightly injured people waiting to have stitches and anti-tetanus injections. She had a quick word with Mrs Pink and Staff Nurse Getty, then flew back to escort her patient to theatre. Sir Donald, Doctor van Sibbelt and their patient had already gone; she cleared up the mess in the bay and turned her attention to helping James. And after that there was the business of clearing up—they were quick at that, but it took time; everything had to be exactly as it was, ready for any kind of emergency once more.

The morning had gone. It was long past the nurses' dinner time, she sent them in ones and twos for their belated meal, and when Staff got back, retired to her office, where old Betsy, the department maid, had taken a tray of coffee and sandwiches. She lingered now, to receive praise from Araminta for the useful part she had played in the morning's work.

'Cups o' tea,' she declared contemptuously, 'and collecting up the dirties—that ain't much, Sister. Not when I seen you and the nurses covered in blood, mopping up and bandaging and giving them nasty jabs.'

She spoke with some relish, for although she was a dear old thing, devoted to Araminta, zealous in her cleaning operations round the department and with a heart of gold, she enjoyed any dramatic occasion.

'Go on with you, Betsy,' said Araminta. 'You know as well as I do that hot tea is one of the quickest ways of helping someone who's had a shock to feel normal again—why, if you hadn't been there with your urn, we should have had twice as much work.'

She took a sip of coffee and bit into a sandwich, and Betsy, looking pleased, pushed the sugar bowl nearer. 'That young man, 'im with the leg orf—is 'e going ter be OK?'

Araminta pushed her cap to the back of her head, allowing a good deal of her golden hair to escape untidily, she pushed that back too rather impatiently. 'I hope so, Betsy.'

Her elderly handmaiden trotted to the door, where she paused to say: 'Well, 'e ought ter get well with Sir Donald tackling 'im. And 'oo was that fine fellow with 'im?'

Araminta declared mendaciously that she didn't know, for if she had said anything else Betsy would have stayed for ever, asking questions in her cockney voice; probably the selfsame questions to which Araminta herself would have liked to know the answers. She sighed and dragged a formidable pile of Casualty cards and notes towards her, and began, between bites and gulps, to enter the morning's work into the Record Book. She had barely started when she was called away to cast an eye over an overdose which had been brought in and who Staff didn't quite like the look of. The man was indeed in a sorry state—they worked on him under James' patient directions and then coped with a sprained ankle, an old lady knocked down by a bus, a child scalded by a kettle of boiling water and a very old man found unconscious by the police, and he was followed by a baby who had swallowed a handful of plastic beads. There was a pause after that, long enough for them to stop for a welcome cup of tea while the two student nurses, back from tea, cleared up once more.

'Quite a day!' observed Araminta, 'and I've got all this wretched writing to do before I can get off duty.' She glanced at her watch. 'It's time for those two to go, anyway—Nurse Carter's on at six, isn't she? and Male

Nurse Pratt—he's good; they both are. A pity Sylvia wasn't here, but we should be all right now.' She crossed her fingers hurriedly as she spoke. 'Oh, lord, I shouldn't have said that.' She poured second cups. 'Get yourself off on time, Dolly.'

'What about you, Sister?' Her faithful right hand looked worried.

'Well, I must get this done before I go, and by the time I'm ready the Night people will be on; they've been promised for an hour earlier, you know—I should get away by seven o'clock at the latest.' She added gloomily: 'Let's hope we'll be slack for a day or two so that you can all get the off-duty you're owed.'

Dolly got up and tidied the cups on to the tray and picked it up. 'That would be nice, but I don't suppose it'll work that way, do you?'

Alone, Araminta buried herself in her papers, only lifting her head to bid good night to the nurses as they came off duty and thank them for their hard work. Mrs Pink had gone at four o'clock and Dolly went last of all, putting her head round the door to tell Araminta that the two evening nurses had reported for duty and that the Accident Room was blessedly free of patients for the moment.

'Good,' said Araminta absent-mindedly. 'Night staff will be on soon now—I'll just about be ready by then.'

She was finished by the time they came, but only just, for she had been interrupted once or twice. She gave her report quickly, changed out of uniform and went thankfully out of the hospital doors. There was still some evening left; she would get into a dressing gown and have her supper round the fire—a bath first, perhaps, so that she could tumble into bed as soon as she had eaten it... Her thoughts were interrupted by Doctor van

Sibbelt's quiet voice. 'Quite a day,' he commented. 'You must be tired.'

Indeed she was; it was sheer weariness which made her snap: 'Don't you know better than to creep up on someone like that? I might have screamed!'

'I'm sorry—you need your supper.' He tucked a hand under her arm and began to walk her down the shabby street. 'I'll get it while you have a bath.'

If he had given her the chance she would have stopped in order to express her opinion of this suggestion, but as it was she did the best she could while he hurried her along. 'I haven't asked you to supper, Doctor. I'm far too tired to entertain anyone—even if I had wanted to do so, and I don't.'

He gave a chuckle. 'Yes, yes,' he said soothingly, 'but I hardly expect to be entertained, merely to see that you get a good supper. Let me have your key.'

Araminta handed it over, aware that she was putting up a poor fight, but he had the advantage of her. Her head was addled with weariness and the thought that she was on duty again at eight o'clock the next morning did nothing to help. She went past him into the tiny hall, to turn sharply when he didn't follow her. Quite forgetful of her peevishness, she cried: 'Oh, you're not going away, are you?' for suddenly the idea of getting her own supper and eating it by herself seemed intolerable.

His voice came reassuringly from the dark outside. 'I'm here, fetching the food.' He came in as he spoke, carrying a large paper bag from Harrods. 'Run along now, there's a good girl, while I open a few tins.'

She had the ridiculous feeling that she had known him all her life; that to allow him—a stranger, well, almost a stranger—to get the supper while she took a bath was a perfectly normal thing to do. She giggled tiredly as, nicely refreshed, she swathed herself in her dressing gown and tied back her hair. Aunt Martha would probably die of shock if she could see her now! Come to think of it, she was a little shocked herself. Something of it must have shown on her face as she went into the sitting room, for Doctor van Sibbelt, carefully opening a bottle of wine, gave her one swift look and said in the most matter-of-fact of voices: 'I don't know about you, but I'm famished. Do you often get a day like this one?'

She sat down in the little tub chair by the fire. 'It's never as bad as today, though we're usually busy enough.'

'Nicely organised, too,' he commented. 'That young chap should be all right—Sir Donald did a splendid job on him.'

'You gave the anaesthetic…'

He put the wine down and started for the kitchen. 'Yes. I'm going to bring in the soup.'

It was delicious—bisque of shrimps. Araminta supped it up, keeping conversation to a minimum, and when he whisked the bowls away and came back with two plates of lemon chicken and a great bowl of crisps, as well as a smaller one of artichoke salad, she sighed her deep pleasure.

'I can't think why you should be so kind,' she exclaimed. 'Are you a Cordon Bleu cook or something?'

He poured their wine. 'My dear girl, I can't boil an egg. I just went along to the food counters and pointed at this and that and then warmed them up on your stove.'

She crunched a handful of crisps. 'Are you on holiday?' she asked as casually as she knew how, and was thwarted when he said carelessly: 'Shall we say combining business with pleasure?' And he had no intention of telling her more than that. His next remark took her completely by surprise: 'You don't fit into the London scene, you know—you looked more at home among the cliffs of Cornwall.'

She remembered with some indignation how austere and unfriendly he had been then and decided not to answer him. He had, after all, given her an excellent supper, even though she hadn't asked for it, and she couldn't repay his kindness with rudeness.

'You like your job?' he wanted to know.

She nibbled a crisp. 'Yes, very much, and I'm very lucky to have this flat.' She spoke with faint challenge, and he smiled a little.

'Er—I'm sure you are. I'll fetch the coffee.'

She watched him go to the kitchen. He was quite something, even though she reminded herself that she didn't care for that type—self-assured, too good-looking by far and with a nasty temper to boot. And he had this peculiar habit of turning up unexpectedly and for no reason at all—and why on earth should he have gone to the trouble of buying supper and cooking it for her? She wasn't the only one who had been overworked that day. Presently, when they had had their coffee, she would find that out, but now she contented herself with: 'Are you a physician?'

He put two lumps of sugar into her mug and four into his own. 'Yes.'

'But you don't work here—in England?' she persisted.

He sat back, crossed one long leg over the other and contemplated his shoes. 'You're very inquisitive,' he observed mildly.

'I am not,' said Araminta hotly. 'You invited yourself

to supper, just like that, and—and you came the other evening, just as though we were lifelong friends, and you expect me to entertain you without knowing the first thing…you might be anyone!'

He put down his mug. 'So I might, I hadn't thought of that. I can assure you that I lead a more or less blameless life, that Sir Donald knows me very well indeed, and that I have no intention of harming you in any way.' He grinned suddenly. 'I have always favoured big dark girls with black eyes…'

Araminta snorted. 'I am not in the least interested in your tastes or habits,' she assured him untruthfully. 'And now would you mind very much if you go? You've been very kind, giving me this nice supper, and I'm most grateful,' then she added with disarming honesty: 'I don't think I like you.'

He disconcerted her by throwing back his head and laughing so loudly that she cried urgently: 'Oh, shush—do think of the neighbours!' She fetched his coat and offered it to him. 'Good night, and thank you again,' she said politely and stood while he slung the coat round his shoulders, which made him seem more enormous than he already was. At the door she asked: 'Why did you come?'

'I wanted to see you again.'

'You said that last time.'

He swooped suddenly and kissed her hard. 'I daresay I shall say it next time, too,' he assured her, and added blandly: 'I would have washed up…'

He had gone, up the area steps and into the dark street, without saying goodnight or goodbye. Araminta stood where she was, staring out into the night, her pretty tired face the picture of astonishment. Presently she went inside and cleared away the remains of their supper and washed the dishes. She did it very carelessly, breaking a mug and two plates, while she urged her tired brain to reflect upon the evening. But she gave up very soon and went to bed; she really was too weary to think straight, the morning would give her more sense. The thought that she might see the doctor again sneaked into the back of her mind and wiped everything else out of it, although she told herself that she couldn't bear him at any price—she would make that quite clear to him the next time they met.

CHAPTER THREE

A GOOD NIGHT'S SLEEP worked wonders. Araminta rose at her usual hour, got her breakfast, tidied her small home and walked briskly to St Katherine's. It was a chilly, grey day and the streets looked drearier than usual, but she didn't notice that. She was wondering, in the light of early morning, how on earth she had allowed herself to be conned into inviting Doctor van Sibbelt to supper. Thinking about it, she was pretty sure that she hadn't. He had invited himself—and he had behaved very strangely; she had been kissed before, but somehow this time she had felt disturbed by it, and that was strange in itself, because she didn't like him. She would take great care to treat him with polite aloofness when next they met.

She entered the Accident Room, carrying on a mythical conversation with him in which he came off very much the worse for wear, and was brought up short by the line of people already in the waiting area. Of course, they would be some of the victims of yesterday's bomb, come for a check-up. A good number of them had been sent to their own doctors for after-care, but there had been several doubtful ones who had been asked to return. Doctor van Sibbelt's handsome features faded at once and stayed that way until she went to her dinner, leaving Sylvia to cope with the few patients who were receiving attention.

Most of her friends were there, consuming their meal with the businesslike speed of those who never have the chance to linger over their food, but they managed to get a good deal of talking done at the same time. Araminta was plied with questions and the conditions of the various patients she had dispatched to the wards the day before were discussed at some length. They were consuming their stewed fruit and custard when someone asked: 'Who was that man with Sir Donald? I saw them coming out of theatre. Didn't you say Sir was with you, Araminta?'

Araminta, her mouth full, nodded.

'And the man with him?'

She nodded again and managed: 'He's a doctor.'

'He's a smasher.' It was the same girl who spoke, one of the junior sisters on Men's Surgical, a pert, pretty girl whom nobody liked very much. 'Did you speak to him?'

'Yes,' said Araminta, 'I asked him if he was going to cut down and he said he'd have a try with a needle first.'

There was a little burst of laughter. 'Do you mean to tell me that he didn't ask you out?' asked the pert girl suspiciously.

'No,' said Araminta, and added quenchingly: 'It was hardly the time or the place, was it?'

Her questioner subsided and they got up from the table in twos and threes and went along to the sitting room in the Home for the last precious ten minutes, to drink their tea in peace before going back to their various jobs.

'I can't stand that girl!' Pamela Carr exclaimed as she

and Araminta walked through the maze of passages to the main wing of the hospital, 'and just my wretched luck to be relieving on Men's Surgical while Sister West's on holiday—the creature seems to think that she knows the lot; its "Sister Carr, do this, Sister Carr, do that".' She sniffed. 'She tints her hair.'

Araminta chuckled. 'I thought she did. I didn't like her either, but cheer up, Pam, think of her face when she discovers that you've been offered Sister West's job when she retires after Christmas. The boot'll be on the other foot then.'

Pam sighed. 'It seems a long way off—ever so many things could happen...'

'Such as what?' Araminta pushed the Accident Room door open. 'You could meet a millionaire who falls for you on sight and carries you off to some gorgeous mansion...'

Her companion laughed. 'I'd like to see it happen! It sounds more like you.'

'I'm not the type. 'Bye for now.'

The afternoon dragged a little. The hospital had been taken off take-in for a couple of days, so that all the emergencies could go to neighbouring hospitals, leaving St Katherine's time to get back into its stride. Araminta had the time now to sit at her desk and make out the off duty for the month ahead, write the nurses' reports, harangue the laundry, the dispensary and the Admissions Office by telephone, and go on a careful inspection of her department. This was something she did regularly, for although she was on excellent terms with her staff, she allowed no slackness. She returned to her desk well satisfied; the place was pristine, she had had time to chat to each member of her staff, arranging for them to take the off duty they had missed, say a few words in the kitchen to Betsy, and go along to X-Ray to iron out one or two awkward situations which had cropped up. It was almost time for her to go to tea, but she decided against it; Dolly could go off duty an hour earlier instead. One of the student nurses had already gone, leaving herself and the junior nurse alone until Sylvia took over at five o'clock. Araminta went to find Dolly and then poked her head round the kitchen door once to ask Betsy to let her have a pot of tea when she had a minute to spare. Well satisfied that she had done her best to make everyone happy, she went along to the end bay where a junior houseman was painstakingly reducing a dislocated shoulder. He had done it very well, she noted, only now he hadn't the faintest idea what to do next. She applied the bandage for him, her unassuming manner leading him to believe that he had allowed her to do it out of the kindness of his heart because she needed the practice.

The little corner shop was still open when she went off duty, so she bought a loaf and a tin of beans and a pound of apples and went home, where, over her simple meal, she found herself wishing that the Dutch doctor was there too, bad temper and all, offering her something tasty from Harrods.

It was several days later that she overheard Sir Donald telling James that Doctor van Sibbelt was back in his own country. It was a pity that they walked away just then and she was unable to hear any more. It was fortunate, though, that that very evening she had agreed to go to the cinema with James. They had time for a cup of coffee before the film started and she led the conversation carefully round to Doctor van Sibbelt, 'What part of Holland does he come from?' she wanted to know in an off-hand way.

'No idea. I don't really know what he does—something in medicine, of course. He comes over here quite a bit, so I hear. His English is pretty good, isn't it?'

'I—yes, I suppose so…'

James rambled on. 'He's rather a splendid-looking chap, I thought—made a great impression on the girls…' He chuckled to himself. 'Not bad, seeing that he's reaching for forty.' The way he said it made it sound like eighty, and Araminta said sharply: 'That's not even middle-aged,' and then hurried on because James had given her a mildly enquiring look: 'Ought we to be going? I'd hate to miss any of the film.'

And that was the last of Doctor van Sibbelt. Or so she told herself.

She went home the following weekend, driving herself in the Mini. It was a splendid morning, although there was a nip in the air which warned her that winter wasn't so very far away. She left early, before the morning traffic piled up, so that she was out of London and on to the M4 while the roads were still fairly quiet. She drove fast, stopping briefly for coffee before turning off the motorway to go across country to Bridgewater. She was a good driver, but if she went through Bristol she would be held up for hours and she knew the quieter country roads very well. At Bridgewater she took the Minehead road and slowed down to enjoy the scenery, and Dunster, when she reached it, was delightfully quiet. She entered the little town on a sigh of pleasure, past the Luttrell Arms and the smalls shops lining the broad main street, with a glimpse of the castle at the end of it, and then past the church and into a narrow lane where the houses, although small, were well kept. At the end of the row, standing a little apart, was her home, just the same as all the others but with a small garden before it. Araminta pulled the Mini into the side of the road and jumped out, running up the path like a small girl to fling herself into Aunt Martha's arms and then embrace her father. And there was Toby to hug too, an elderly non-descript cat who had walked in one day years ago and had been a close member of the household ever since. He sat on her lap, purring, while she drank the coffee her aunt insisted she needed before they had their lunch, and presently she went upstairs to her small, rather dark, room, with its shelves full of china ornaments and the bits and pieces she had collected since she was a very small girl, and its narrow bed with its faded eiderdown. She tidied herself slowly, savouring the quiet and the delicious smells coming from the kitchen. Aunt Martha might look like a straightlaced dowager, but she was a dream of a cook.

It was after lunch, when they had washed up and were sitting round the fire, her aunt with her knitting, her father with his pipe and a massive book at his elbow and Araminta sitting between them with Toby in her lap once more, that the name of Doctor van Sibbelt cropped up. They had been talking about their holiday and it was Aunt Martha who remarked on his charm of manner as she went on to say: 'And did he go to see you, child? I gave him your address; he seemed anxious to let you know about that little girl-Mary Rose.'

'Oh, yes—he called one evening.' Araminta had her voice casual.

'Very thoughtful of him—a kind, considerate man,' pronounced her aunt. 'You agreed with me, William?'

Mr Shaw nodded. 'A first-class sailor, too.' He smiled at his daughter, and as they both expected her to contribute her share of his praises, she said: 'Yes, well… As a matter of fact, he's a doctor. I daresay you know. He lives in Holland—he went back…'

She hadn't meant to mention that fact. Now they would ask any number of questions, bless them. But she need not have worried, for her father exclaimed: 'Good heavens, that reminds me, I had a long letter from your cousin Thomas this very morning. My elder sister's boy, if you remember, my dear. He's been married some years now and he must be ten years or more older than you—more,' he paused to think. 'I can't quite remember in which year he was born…'

'That doesn't matter,' interrupted Aunt Martha firmly. 'Tell her about the letter.'

'Ah, yes. He went into the Civil Service and has been living for several years in Amsterdam—something to do with the Common Market. There's a boy, he must be about ten years old.' He paused again, this time to re-light his pipe while his listeners waited with outward patience. 'Thelma, his wife—perhaps you remember her?—is very ill; leukaemia, and it seems she can't live long, poor girl. Thomas asks if you would go over to Amsterdam and look after her and run the house. It would be a question of a month or so—even weeks. Thelma doesn't speak the language very well and doesn't want anyone in the house. Thomas thought of you.' He looked at Araminta over his spectacles. 'I daresay he doesn't know that you have a very good job; after all, we don't correspond very much. I daresay you don't remember him at all…'

'Oh, yes I do, Father. Not very tall and going a little bald and he was pompous—poor little man.' She returned her father's look steadily. 'You'd like me to go, wouldn't you, Father?'

He smiled. 'His mother was my favourite sister and we were very close, though I can't say I ever took to Thomas. I leave it to you, my dear, but it would be very nice if you could get leave from the hospital. He doesn't mention paying you and I suppose if you could get leave it would be unpaid? There is such an arrangement?'

'I think so, but I'm not sure for how long I could go. If I got a couple of weeks, would that help? Just long enough for Thomas to make some other arrangement? If Thelma is very ill she might have to go into hospital, or if she's able, be brought back to England.'

'Now that's an idea,' agreed Aunt Martha, 'and perhaps if you were there with her, you could persuade her. Does she really have to go into hospital?'

'When she becomes very ill, yes, although she could get worse suddenly before she could be moved. I don't know anything about it, but if she's fit enough and the doctors there would agree to it, I could bring her back—has she got any family?'

'None,' said her father, 'more's the pity.'

'And the boy?'

'Well, they've been there three years or more and of course he goes to a Dutch school—probably Thomas wouldn't want to take him away.'

Araminta was aware that she was being looked at intently. Her father and her aunt were both sweeties, but they still lived in a different age. They had made sacrifices in their youth; probably done a great many things they hadn't wanted to do because it had been their duty, and they couldn't conceive of anyone doing other than that. Probably, she thought wryly, they thought that she wouldn't mind jeopardizing her job—her future, even, in order to do her duty by the family. Any minute now they would remind her that blood was thicker than water. She said quietly: 'I'll go and see about it when I get back—will that be time enough? I'm sure something could be arranged.'

She was rewarded by their relieved smiles.

The weekend went far too quickly. Araminta went to church on Sunday morning and then stood about in the churchyard, talking to the people she had known all her life, and in the afternoon, her elderly relations nicely settled by the fire, she put on an old tweed coat, tied a scarf over her hair and walked briskly through the village and down to the water. The weather was still clear and sunny, Wales seemed very close with only the Bristol Channel between them. She walked along the rough sand, kicking up the stones, her hands in her pockets, and thought about going to Holland. It would be fun to see another country; true, she had been to France several times, but Holland seemed more foreign, probably because she knew very little about it—not that she would get much time to herself to explore, she thought gloomily; running Thomas's house, looking after Thelma and keeping an eye on the boy would surely keep her fully occupied.

She turned for home and found herself wondering whereabouts Doctor van Sibbelt lived—Holland was such a very small country, they might bump into each other. She stopped to throw stones into the water, frowning. She seemed to remember reading somewhere that Holland was very densely populated, which made their chance of meeting amongst the teeming millions even less likely.

She went to the office when she got back on Tuesday morning. The Accident Room was busy, but not so busy that Staff Nurse Getty couldn't manage very well for half an hour; besides, since the bomb, she had been sent two extra nurses. Miss Best, the Principal Nursing Officer, heard her out without interruption and then sat frowning down at the papers before her. At length she said: 'Well, Sister Shaw, I won't deny that your request comes at a very awkward time—just when we need every nurse we have, and you are invaluable to us, you know, but I don't see how I can refuse you. I suggest that you have three weeks unpaid leave and if circumstances allow you will return within that time, and if for any reason you are unable to do so, then we must review the situation. When do you wish to go?'

Araminta thought. 'I have to write to my cousin and find out when he wants me—imagine that will take a day or so. If I am prepared to go in three days' time—just in case he telephones—and go on working until I hear for certain. Would that do?'

Miss Best nodded a majestic head. 'That seems a sensible idea,' she agreed. 'You will of course return as soon as possible, Sister Shaw?'

'Yes, of course, Miss Best—only supposing my cousin's wife should need me longer than the three weeks—I mean, for a much longer period?'

Miss Best eyed her morosely across the desk. 'Then I shall have no choice but to fill your post—you see, I cannot afford to hold it open, much though I should regret having to replace you, my dear.' She added bracingly: 'But I trust that this won't occur, and if it should, I shall do my utmost to help you, you may depend on that.' Her severe face broke into a smile. 'Let us look on the bright side and hope that you will return very shortly.'

And that was all very well, thought Araminta confusedly, but it might not be the bright side for Thelma. She made a suitable reply and went back to the Accident Room, which, in her absence, had become a hive of industry, so that it was impossible to tell anyone that she would be going away very shortly. She wrote to her father during her delayed dinner time, and wrote to Thomas too, thinking as she did so that she wasn't going to enjoy his company very much, but if Thelma was very ill, she wouldn't have much time to spend with him. Besides, there was the boy whose name she had forgotten to ask. She sighed as she stuck on the stamps. She might have made her father and Aunt Martha happy, and possibly Thomas, but she certainly hadn't followed her own inclinations. She went back to her work, and when there was a breathing space, told Dolly and Mrs Pink, who promptly offered to increase her hours of duty while she was away—a kind gesture, seeing that she had a husband and two children to look after as well as doing her work as a staff nurse at the hospital.

She received a pompously worded telegram two days later, urging her to leave for Amsterdam at the earliest moment, and the following morning, with the good wishes of her friends ringing in her ears, she was on her way. She had decided to fly to Holland, though it would have been nicer to have taken the Mini, but the chance to get out on her own would be slight and it would have been a waste of money and effort. Besides, it was only for a week or two, sooner than that perhaps, if she could persuade the doctors to let Thelma return to England.

She followed the other passengers off the KLM plane at Schiphol and hoped that there would be someone to meet her. There wasn't, so she stood around for a little while until it became evident that Thomas hadn't been able to get to the airport, and in all fairness to him, she hadn't asked to be met, merely said at what time she would arrive, so she went outside and got on a bus, in which she was whisked to the city in a very short space of time, and found herself outside the KLM offices where she got herself a taxi, showed Thomas's address to the driver, and then sat back to enjoy the ride. For the first ten minutes or so she gazed enchanted from the taxi window, trying to look at everything at once—the tall, gabled houses, the bustling streets, and the glimpses of steel grey water as they crossed the canals. But presently they turned away from the city's heart, driving now through narrow streets lined with blocks of modern flats, red brick and functional. Araminta hoped fervently that Thomas didn't live in one of them, and breathed a sigh of relief when the street merged into a wide thoroughfare with a broad canal running alongside it, and the other taken up by more flats—but they weren't as high as the previous ones, and they had wide windows filled with flowers and handsome entrances as well as grass lawns between the blocks, laid out with trees and shrubs which, even at the end of autumn, looked pleasant enough. Perhaps Thomas and his family lived in one of these.

It seemed that he did; the taxi-driver slithered to a halt before the entrance to a block half way down the street, got out, carried her case into the hall for her, waited patiently while she found the right money, and bade her a cheerful goodbye. She felt a little lost without him; she quite understood that Thomas might not have been able to meet her at Schiphol, but surely he could have been on the look-out for her arrival? She stood looking around her. The hall was square with a staircase in one corner and two lifts, side by side, and it was very quiet. For all she knew the building might have been empty. She went over to the lifts and tried, with no success at all, to decipher the notices beside them, and muttering crossly because she couldn't understand a word of them, got into one and pressed the button for the third floor. Thomas's number was one hundred and thirty-five, and she had to start somewhere. The third floor landing looked very like the entrance hall and was just as silent; the flat numbers went no higher than one hundred. Araminta got back into the lift again and pressed the button to the fifth floor, and this time she was lucky; the flat was at the end of a long corridor, well carpeted and very clean. When she rang the bell, the door was opened by a small boy who stared at her for a long moment and then said in an accusing way: 'You're Araminta—we've been expecting you.'

It was on the tip of her tongue to point out that it didn't look much like it to her, but she smiled instead, wishing she knew his name, and contented herself with a cheerful 'Hullo.'

'Father's waiting for you in his study,' the boy told her. 'He's stayed home until you got here.'

She bit back the words teetering on her tongue. It would never do to start off on the wrong foot; probably Thomas was beside himself with worry and anxiety. But when she was ushered into a small dark room facing the front door, to find Thomas sitting behind a desk much too large for him and looking incredibly pompous, she was inclined to change her mind about that. He didn't look anxious about anything, only annoyed and impatient. And his greeting was hardly what she had expected, for he pushed aside some papers before him and without bothering to get out of his chair, said: 'Bertram saw your taxi arrive. If I had had the time to write to you, I should have told you to take the bus, it would have cost far less—as it is, you've taken a good deal longer than I should have thought necessary.'

Araminta chose a chair and sat down. She said in a calm, cool voice which hid her rage very well indeed: 'It seems that you've changed your mind, Thomas. From your telegram I gathered that you wanted me to come and help Thelma—probably you've made other plans and no longer wish me to stay with you.'

He looked so astonished and dismayed that she almost laughed. 'Why should you say that?' he demanded.

'You don't appear to be at all pleased to see me. You knew what time I was arriving at the airport, but I hardly expected you to meet me there. I thought you would be looking after Thelma—and really, the least you could have done, when Bertram saw my taxi arriving, was to have come down and met me. Instead of which you sit there as though you were interviewing a new maid—perhaps it's living in Holland,' she added reflectively.

Thomas looked as though he would choke; his face went a rich plum colour and he gobbled. He got up from his chair and came round the desk, a short, stout man, not even middle-aged. But he was, she decided judicially, a man who had never been anything else…'I'm sorry,' he said stiffly. 'I have a great deal of work on my mind—an important job, you understand; extra time on committees, and so on…'

'And Thelma?' prompted Araminta.

'Naturally, although I fancy that she takes advantage of her sickly disposition. I'm aware that she's ill, but she's still a young woman—to resign herself to the life of an invalid seems to me to be quite unnecessary.'

'Well…!' Araminta breathed deeply, biting off the words she had been about to utter and contenting herself with a fervent: 'I'm glad I came.'

She was misunderstood, for Thomas said graciously: 'Amsterdam is a splendid city in which to live, and as you see, I have an excellent flat. And I own a Mercedes.' He allowed himself a smile. 'I venture to think that my work is by no means unimportant here.'

'Where's Thelma?' asked Araminta, her patience at such a low ebb that she very nearly reached and thumped her cousin.

'She's probably in the bedroom.'

'Then since I'm here—at your request, Thomas—to do what I can for her, I'll go and meet her.'

He preceded her to the door. 'Splendid—now that you're here, Cousin Araminta, I shall leave for my office.'

She paused outside the door. 'You come home to lunch?'

'No—Thelma usually gets herself a little something.'

'And Bertram?'

'He has a midday snack with the children of a colleague of mine, and returns home about four o'clock.'

'And you? When do you get back?'

He smiled thinly. 'Dear me, what an inquisition I usually return about six o'clock—I have various people to meet…'

She cut him short mercilessly. 'And who cooks the evening meal and does the shopping for it?'

'Thelma is quite able…and there's a woman who comes in to clean—she'll shop if she's asked.'

Araminta gave him such a ferocious look that he

took a step backwards and then hastily opened a door in the hall, saying as he did so: 'Here's Cousin Araminta, my dear. I'll leave you to renew your acquaintance and go to the office, I've already missed several hours' work,' he sounded accusing. 'I'll take Bertram with me and drop him off at school, it's very nearly time for his midday break.'

He had gone before Araminta could say anything more, closing the door behind him, and leaving her to cross the large, expensively furnished room to the chair by one of the windows where Thelma sat.

During her years in hospital Araminta had learned to school her pretty features into a smiling calmness, however horrifying or shocking the sights she had met with. She was glad of that now, for Thelma shocked her. She hadn't seen her for more than ten years, it was true, but this white-faced, thin woman, sitting so tiredly, wasn't anything like the Thelma she had known. She bent and kissed her gently, saying cheerfully: 'Heavens, what ages since we last met, and what a great deal we have to talk about. Look, I'm going to put my things in my room and make us a drink.'

Thelma smiled then. 'You didn't mind me not coming to meet you? I get tired, you know, it's this anaemia, I suppose. Thomas said he would see to everything—he's shown you your room, I expect?' She paused and added hesitantly: 'He was angry when the doctor said I ought to have someone to help me around the house and be with me when I go out—I'm afraid to go alone, you see—so silly, but sometimes I feel faint. Wasn't it lucky that Thomas remembered that you were a nurse? I was so glad when I heard that you were coming—I'm a great expense, you see; he said if you didn't come I should have to manage, for he couldn't afford to pay anyone.'

Araminta went on smiling while she boiled with rage. Her cousin's meanness made her feel sick, and that he should actually be a member of the family made her feel even sicker. She managed a cheerful reply and went in search of her room—small and overfurnished with the same expensive modern furniture—and then went to inspect the kitchen, where she made a large pot of tea, buttered some toast, and carried the tray back to the bedroom. Tomorrow, she promised herself, things would be different.

Over their tea, Thelma began to talk. She got tired and breathless doing it, but it was obviously such a relief that Araminta didn't interrupt her. She had this anaemia, she explained, and she had gone to the hospital once or twice, besides having a very good doctor who gave her pills, only despite these she felt so tired, and then Thomas was so easily annoyed. 'He thinks there's no need for me to go to the hospital, the last twice he rang up and cancelled the appointment—you see, he has so little time to take me. He has a car, but he needs it for the office, and besides that he's on several committees and goes out a good deal in the evenings.' She added wistfully: 'I should like to go out sometimes—with Bertram, you know, he's getting a big boy and I sometimes think…' She paused. 'Thomas has no time…'

Araminta sniffed delicately. Thomas, in her opinion, was just about the worst husband in the world. 'When do you go to the hospital for your next check-up?' she wanted to know.

'In four days' time—Thomas asked them to put it off for two weeks. I can't manage to go there by myself, you see, and it wasn't convenient for him to take me. He told them that I was quite well. You see, he'd just remembered you and hoped you would be here to take me.' Thelma's eyes filled with tears. 'I'm such a nuisance,' she whispered.

'Oh, no, you're not,' declared Araminta vigorously. 'What's more, you're going to feel better in no time at all—I don't think you've been eating enough for a start, and there's no reason why we shouldn't take a short walk every day—the doctor won't know you when he sees you at the hospital.'

And that was true enough, for sadly, unless she was very much mistaken, Thelma was very ill indeed.

She tackled Thomas about it that evening. She had spent the rest of the day helping Thelma to dress and then sit her comfortably in the living room while she took stock of the kitchen once more. Apparently she was expected to get an evening meal ready as well as cut sandwiches for Bertram, who came back from school famished. He wasn't a nice boy, she decided, for a ten-year-old he was far too precocious. She had told him off roundly for coming in with muddy boots and sent him to take them off and put on slippers and wash his hands besides, and his surprise had been quite ludicrous. Evidently he had been doing more or less what he liked around the place, and he treated his mother with an off-hand casualness which annoyed her very much.

After they had all had tea together, Araminta had suggested that he got on with his homework, and very much at a loss as to how to treat her, he had done so meekly enough, leaving her free to prepare a meal for the evening and resume conversation with Thelma.

Thomas had come home about six o'clock, greeted

his wife with a brief peck on her cheek, nodded to Araminta, remarking that she had probably had an enjoyable day, and retired to his study, whence she followed him without delay. Determined to keep her temper at all costs, she said urgently: 'Thomas, you do realize that Thelma is very ill?'

He fussed with the papers on his desk and muttered: 'I'm a very busy man—some other time…'

'Now,' said Araminta, 'and don't talk a lot of rot about being busy, because you're not. And while I'm here I'll make one or two things clear. I came because you sent for me urgently, not to be an unpaid house-keeper while you sit behind that desk doing nothing, but to look after Thelma, who heaven knows needs all the care she can get. I'd imagined that you would be beside yourself with worry about her,' she went on, 'but you're not. But that's not my business, though it is my business to see that she gets good food, proper rest, and gentle exercise, which means that you'll have to hire a taxi every afternoon to take us to the nearest park and back again. And she needs things to make her feel better, even if she isn't—champagne, and not just half a bottle, but each day—flowers in her room, anything she fancies to eat…'

He was plum coloured again. 'My dear Cousin Araminta, the expense!'

Her voice trembled with her effort to keep it matter-of-fact. 'You've got me for nothing, think what you're saving on a nurse's fees, besides,' she added soberly, 'it won't be for long, you know.'

She turned for the door and paused there. 'And another thing, why did you cancel her appointment at the hospital? Don't you know it's vital that she should be seen regularly?'

He didn't look at her. 'It's difficult for me to get enough time—she wasn't ill, only tired and a bit pale.'

'I suppose you told the doctor that she was doing fine.'

'I said she was feeling much better…'

'Pah!' snapped Araminta, and went out, leaving the door open. There was a great deal she longed to say, but there was Thelma to think of.

She lay awake that night, wondering if she had been too hasty in her judgement of Thomas. She had been tired and uncertain of what she would find and intolerant because of it—she would apologise in the morning. She slept fitfully on the thought.

She was roused just before six o'clock by Thomas. Thelma had been sick after a bad night, and perhaps Araminta would go and freshen her up. 'I need my sleep,' he explained grumpily. 'I shall go to the spare room—don't call me until eight o'clock.'

Araminta, looking like a sleepy angel, gave him a non-angelic look. 'I shan't call you at all,' she assured him coldly, 'and don't expect me to get your breakfast, either—it's Thelma I'm looking after.' She sailed past him, her beautiful little nose lifted, and went into Thelma's room and closed the door.

She was as good as her word. She attended to her patient's wants, stayed with her until she fell into exhausted sleep, and then went back to her own room and dozed until the banging of the front door roused her. Thomas had gone, taking Bertram with him and leaving chaos in the kitchen. Despite that, she and Thelma spent a pleasant day together, and Araminta, who could cook quite nicely when she had a mind to, was delighted to see the invalid eat at least some of the dainty lunch she had prepared, and in the afternoon, nicely rested,

Thelma, warmly wrapped against the wintry wind, and with Araminta's arm to support her, went for a short taxi ride and an even shorter walk in the neighbouring park before returning home to tea and toast before Bertram got home. Araminta was pleased to see that he wiped his boots carefully as he came in, although his manner towards his mother left a lot to be desired.

Thomas was, if possible, even more pompous than before when he got home. Araminta ignored this, however, merely asking him if he had remembered to bring the champagne and reminding him that he owed her the taxi fare from their afternoon's outing. He paid up with ill grace and muttered something about the champagne which she didn't quite hear. 'I can always telephone an order for it and have the bill sent here,' said Araminta sweetly.

The next two days followed the same pattern. By the fourth morning Araminta told herself that Thelma had improved just a little. She was eating—not nearly enough, but it was a start, and she was certainly brighter in herself, even talking about a few hours' shopping, and Araminta had entered into her plans wholeheartedly. Probably their day at the shops would never materialise, but Thelma was enjoying the prospect of it. It seemed only too evident that she had had very little pleasure in the last few months.

They arrived in good time for Thelma's eleven o'clock appointment, so that there was time to look around them while they waited. The hospital was old, but the outpatients' department had been modernised and made very comfortable in the process. It was, naturally enough, packed, but Araminta would have been surprised if it had been otherwise. There seemed to be plenty of nurses too. She watched them with interest as they went about their work, quite unaware of the glances she was attracting to her own person, and even if she had been she would have thought little of it. She had accepted her honey-coloured hair as something a little out of the common at which other people stared, years ago. She turned to smile at Thelma, already tiring, but cheerful still.

'Not much longer, I think—you're all right?'

'I'm fine, and I don't mind waiting, it's nice to see so many people. I've loved these last few days—it's been such fun with you here.' Thelma smiled slowly. 'You do look nice in that suit.' She studied Araminta's outfit, and indeed it was worth a look; its russet brown, flecked with tawny orange and complemented by Araminta's best leather handbag and gloves, was decidedly eye-catching, as were her elegant brogue shoes.

'You don't look so bad yourself,' countered Araminta. 'I like that blue coat. When we go shopping let's look for a dress to match it—corduroy perhaps, or fine wool…' She launched into an undemanding chat about clothes which filled in the time nicely until their turn came at last. But when the nurse called Thelma's name and came towards them, Thelma said urgently: 'Araminta, you must come with me—I can't…I…'

'Why not?' asked Araminta matter-of-factly, and tucked a firm hand under her arm, glancing at the nurse as she did so. The nurse smiled and nodded and led the way past the rows of other patients to one of the doors facing them, and opened it.

The man behind the desk was young still, with a serious face and a quiet voice. He wished Thelma a sober good morning and looked enquiringly at

Araminta, who said quickly: 'I hope you don't mind, Mrs Shaw asked me to come in with her.'

He nodded. 'You are of her family?'

'I'm her husband's cousin—I'm staying with her for a little while.'

He nodded again and bent to read the papers before him. 'You should have come two weeks ago,' he stated, and listened while Thelma explained, not very clearly. When she had finished, he said: 'I should like to examine you, Mrs Shaw, and take a blood test, for that is long overdue. We will do that first.'

He took his time with her and Araminta liked the way he put his questions, careful not to allow Thelma to guess how ill she was. He was still writing notes when the nurse came back with the path lab results of the blood count. The doctor read it with the expressionless face Araminta had come to know so well, and laid it on one side. It was only after he had written another line or two that he said casually: 'Well, I think it's time the professor saw you again, Mrs Shaw—it's, let me see, two months since you saw him, isn't it?' I'll see if he can spare a minute or two.'

He gathered up his notes, nodded to the nurse and disappeared, and Thelma said worriedly: 'Oh, dear, why do I have to see the specialist? Am I worse?'

'Of course not,' said Araminta soothingly. 'It's just a routine thing, love. You see, you're under this consultant, whoever he is, but he can't see all his patients every week. He sees them the first time, decides what's to be done for them, tells his registrars the treatment he wants done and then casts his eye over them every month or so.'

She turned round as the door opened, to admit the doctor who had been examining Thelma. With him was Doctor van Sibbelt.

CHAPTER FOUR

ARAMINTA SAT with her head over one shoulder, staring at him, her mouth very slightly open, feeling she had just travelled downwards in a lift very fast. She had wondered if she would ever see him again, and had even admitted to herself that it would be rather exciting to do so; only this was more than exciting. She closed her mouth and eyed him in silence.

Doctor van Sibbelt wished Thelma a pleasant good morning, said briefly and disappointingly: 'So we meet again, Miss Shaw,' and glanced at the notes he was carrying. After a moment he went on: 'Mrs Shaw, I think that, as you are here, it would be a good idea for you to have a blood transfusion—you won't object to that?' He paused to smile at her with great charm. 'It would save you coming back this afternoon, would it not? and it will take only a short time. After an hour's rest you will be able to go home.'

Thelma looked worried. 'Oh—must I really? Thomas doesn't know—shall I feel all right afterwards?' She added uncertainly: 'I thought that those pills I've been taking…wouldn't they do as well?'

His voice was reassuringly calm and decidedly

soothing. 'They have done you a great deal of good, but if you have this transfusion, it will do the work of any number of pills in a fraction of the time. You will feel the benefit almost immediately.' He smiled again and questioned gently: 'You are becoming a little tired lately?'

'Well, yes.'

'I can promise you that you will have a great deal more energy, Mrs Shaw. If you would go with Nurse—just across the passage. Miss Shaw can wait for you.'

His manner was quiet but compelling. Thelma cast a look at Araminta, who smiled and nodded encouragingly, and followed the nurse from the room. The door had barely closed behind them when Doctor van Sibbelt muttered something to the registrar, who went out too. Only then did he sit himself down.

'Perhaps you can explain why Mrs Shaw hasn't been for her check-ups?' he observed coldly. 'I see that she has missed the last two, and over the period she has been coming to us she has missed several more—and this last one,' he picked up the path lab form and waved it at her, 'her haemoglobin is thirty-two per cent. We'll give her a transfusion and that will keep her on her feet a little longer, but she will need another in a few days' time, and then another and another...a rapid deterioration.' He sighed. 'Didn't you see? You are a nurse...'

'Of course I saw! I arrived four days ago and found her sitting in a chair in her room, too tired to dress herself. My cousin, her husband, refuses to admit that she's ill. She's been managing somehow, but she hasn't bothered to eat and she hadn't been out for weeks...'

'They are poor people?'

'Certainly not—Thomas runs a Mercedes and the flat

is in the Berestraat, which is quite a good neighbourhood, so I'm told, and it's stuffed with expensive furniture.'

'She should have a companion or daily nurse—we advised that some time ago, I cannot think why…' He paused at Araminta's impatient little snort, and then: 'Start at the beginning and tell me all about it,' he invited.

She hesitated, but only for a moment. The ill-tempered man who had rescued her in Cornwall had been wholly swallowed up by this quiet, well-dressed man who was so sure of himself. She could think of no one to whom she would rather unburden herself. She drew a deep breath and plunged into her sorry tale. When she had finished she made a small choking sound and declared furiously: 'Men!'

Her listener hadn't interrupted her once, but now he said with the faintest of smiles. 'We aren't all Thomases, my dear girl.' His tone became brisk. 'We have to think what is best for Mrs Shaw—I think you should take her home presently and put her to bed and give her her supper there. In the morning she will feel very much better, but as you know, that isn't going to last long, but while it does, I suggest that you get her out as much as she feels she can manage—let her feel, she's leading a normal life as far as it's possible. I'll arrange for her to come in for another transfusion on—let me see—two days' time, and in the meantime I'll get my secretary to make an appointment for her husband to see me.' He got up and crossed the room and stood looking down at her. 'I'm afraid Mrs Shaw's days are numbered,' he said gently.

Araminta nodded, not looking at him. 'Yes, I—I guessed that. I'm glad I came.'

He stared down at her downbent head. 'So am I, although it was inevitable.' He didn't attempt to explain this remark but looked at his watch. 'Mrs Shaw won't be ready for almost two hours,' he paused for so long that she looked questioningly at him. 'I have two more patients to see and in rather less than that time I have a lecture to give. Will you have something to eat with me presently? If you like to go back to the waiting room?'

She was surprised to find how pleased she was at his invitation, but all the same she hesitated. 'It's very kind of you, but I'm sure you have a great deal to do, and I don't in the least mind just sitting and waiting for Thelma.' Araminta hoped her voice sounded more convinced of this than she felt; apparently it didn't, for he took no notice of this at all, merely opening the door for her and repeating: 'About twenty minutes, then,' in such bland certainty that she found herself saying yes quite meekly.

The waiting room had emptied of the morning clinics and was rapidly filling again for the afternoon session. She sat quietly, taking stock of all that was going on around her, telling herself that she was really very foolish to feel so excited at the prospect of an hour of Doctor van Sibbelt's company, especially as she didn't like him. Being an honest girl, she had to admit to herself that that wasn't true any more; she wouldn't quite admit to liking him, but she did admit to a lively interest in him. Perhaps she would have the chance to ask a few pertinent questions over their meal—where he lived, whether he was married—surely he would be?—if he had children… Her reflections were interrupted by his arrival, and she watched him covertly as he came without haste across the vast room, trying to discover in this distinguished-looking man some remnant of the arrogant, faintly mocking giant who had offered to paint her bookshelves for her, and most surprisingly, cooked supper for her, too. But there was no trace. He greeted her casually, led her through OPD and out into the chilly grey day, and walked her down a narrow side street and into a small coffee shop, already half full. It wasn't at all what she had expected, for somehow he fitted into her daydreams of hothouse flowers, Rolls-Royces and champagne, but she was content enough to sit down on a high stool at the counter and cast a hungry eye over the menu.

'Coffee?' he suggested, and when she nodded, 'And how about a *kaas broodje* and a salad?' and when she nodded again, gave the order to the girl behind the counter and sat himself down beside her. He took up a great deal of room; what with a wall on one side of her and him on the other, Araminta was sadly squashed, but somehow she didn't mind at all.

'This is a splendid place in which to talk,' observed her companion, 'it's so noisy and everyone is in a hurry—now tell me about yourself.'

Their coffee had arrived. Araminta poured cream into it and stirred in the sugar before she said: 'There's nothing more to tell.'

'You left a great many gaps,' he pointed out. 'Let's fill them in: do you intend to go back to St Katherine's?'

'Well, I've been given unpaid leave for three weeks—I've had almost a week of that.' She took a bite of her roll and munched contentedly.

'And after that?' prompted her companion.

'My post will be filled.'

'I see—probably I could arrange for a nurse to take care of Mrs Shaw if you want to return before then.'

She took another bite and said with her mouth full:

'Oh, I couldn't do that! Thomas wouldn't pay for anyone, you know.'

'He doesn't—forgive me-pay you?'

'Heavens, no. So you see I must stay now I'm here, especially as Thelma…I can always get another job.' She made her voice cheerful, although the idea of packing up her little flat and finding fresh work wasn't a pleasing one.

'You would miss your friends there, and your work.' He smiled at her, his face very close so that she could see how dark his eyes were. 'Have another roll and some more coffee?'

'Please.' She watched him give the order, admiring his good looks.

'As I was saying, you will miss your friends—I daresay you went out a great deal?'

'Well, yes—I suppose I did.'

'Dinner at the Savoy, orchids and a Rolls to take you there?' he asked with faint mockery, coming too close to her daydreams.

She poured more cream into the fresh cup of coffee he had just handed her. 'Don't be silly—housemen haven't that kind of money. It was mostly egg and chips and very nice too.'

He grinned. 'And did you expect orchids and champagne and quantities of red plush today?'

Araminta put down her roll and gave him a direct look; she was nothing if not honest, it had never occurred to her to be anything else with him. 'Yes, I did—oh, not the orchids, but perhaps a little red plush. You don't—that is, one doesn't expect a consultant to nip across the road for a roll and coffee.' She frowned quite fiercely. 'But before you say something scathing, let me tell you that I'm not in the least disappointed—it's the company, not the food.'

The mocking smile was back again. 'You've stolen my lines, Araminta.'

She went a bright and very becoming pink. 'You're extremely rude! I was actually beginning to like you, but I see now that you're exactly the same as you were when we met…'

'Do tell me.' He sounded amused and not in the least repentant.

'Bad-tempered and impatient and laughing at me.' She drank the rest of her coffee and said in a small, polite voice: 'Thank you for my lunch,' and put out a hand to pick up her purse, but his own large one came down, very gently, on to it.

'I'm all those things, and more,' he told her quietly, 'but could you not like me a little despite them?'

She sat looking at his hand; it felt cool and strong, cherishing hers in its grasp—the hand of someone who would help her if ever she needed it. She said uncertainly: 'I don't understand you, or know anything about you, but I do like you.'

The hand tightened just a little. 'Good,' said the doctor, 'and you're not feeling hurt because you had coffee and *Kaas broodjes* instead of champagne and red plush?'

She tugged at her hand and found it fast held. 'Of course I'm not hurt, and if I had been you I wouldn't have wasted my money on an expensive lunch with someone I hardly knew—you could put it to better use for your wife and children.'

His eyes danced with amusement, although he answered gravely; 'But I have no wife and as far as I know, no children.'

'Oh, well—aren't you even engaged?'

'No, and I think that when I do marry I shan't want to waste time over an engagement.'

'That's arrogant of you—why, the girl might not like that at all.'

'Ah, but the girl I intend to marry will.'

It was strange how deflated Araminta felt at the thought of him marrying, silly too, she told herself sharply, and suggested that it was time for her to fetch Thelma. The deflation was completed by his readiness to go back to the hospital immediately. They parted in OPD and she thanked him once more for her lunch, to be utterly disconcerted when he remarked blandly: 'What a very pretty girl you are—I really think we must have the orchids and red plush together, don't you?'

For some reason his words infuriated her. He was adding her to his list of casual girl-friends, was he? And what about the poor girl he presumably intended marrying? 'How kind,' she told him haughtily, 'but I don't think I want to, thanks.'

He smiled down at her, not in the least put out. 'You are a very unusual girl, and of course you don't like me quite enough yet, do you?'

He walked away and was at once immersed in conversation with a harassed nurse bearing an armful of notes. Araminta watched him look at the clock and then stride through the swing doors. He didn't look round, but she hadn't really expected him to, so that the disappointment she felt was really rather silly.

Thelma, more animated than she had been since Araminta's arrival, and with faintly pink cheeks which made her look much younger, was just ready. Araminta took her home, joining in her companion's gay chatter with a cheerfulness which hid the knowledge that within a very short time Thelma would feel as ill as she had done previously, but at least she could enjoy herself while she felt able to. Rather recklessly, Araminta told the taxi driver to take them as near as he could to the Kalverstraat and wait for them there. Vroom and Dreesman, a large department store, was at the very end of the shopping street; they would only need to walk a very few yards to reach it. The driver was an obliging man, he got out of his cab and gave Thelma an arm across the street and they gained the shop without trouble. It took Thelma only fifteen minutes to find and choose the blue dress she had set her heart on; they were back in the taxi and on the way home in no time at all, and once indoors, Araminta lost no time in putting her to bed with a cup of tea and the injunction to have a nap while she prepared the evening meal before Thomas got home.

Actually, it was he who looked in need of her care when she presented him with the bill for the day's activities. He went an alarming puce, and was in fact so incensed with her wanton spending of his money that he had no time or inclination to worry about Thelma. Araminta saw that it would be hopeless to try and make him understand; perhaps Doctor van Sibbelt would be able to do that. He ate his dinner in a stony silence, declared that he had a committee meeting to attend, and left the house, leaving Araminta to urge Bertram to his bed and then spend a cosy half hour with Thelma, until the invalid dozed off, happier than she had been for a long time.

She stayed happy for the next two days, although on the third morning, when she was due at the hospital again, she was noticeably tired. She answered the sober-faced young doctor's careful questioning cheerfully enough, submitted her finger for the routine prick, and then went off with the nurse to have her second transfusion. When she had gone Araminta got up to go too, but the doctor stopped her.

'The professor wishes that I should tell you how Mrs Shaw progresses. I am afraid that today's results are not good—twenty-nine per cent, despite her previous blood transfusion. She is now gravely ill, but I think that she must not be told of this.' He looked earnestly at her. 'You agree?'

'Yes, I do. She's been very happy—she thinks she's getting better…' Araminta stopped to steady her voice. 'Only I can't make her husband understand.'

'That has been the difficulty with us. The professor tells me that he is seeing Mr Shaw today, perhaps he will be able to explain. In the meantime, Mrs Shaw must lead a quiet life, you understand that? Let her sit up, if she wishes, but that must be all. There will be another transfusion very shortly, but she will be fetched by ambulance. The professor will arrange with Mr Shaw that he is to call his own doctor should Mrs Shaw become worse, and he will be asked to give a report by telephone each day. The end sometimes comes suddenly.' He gave her a kindly smile. 'You have met their house doctor? Doctor de Vos.'

'I've never seen him, although I seem to remember my cousin talking to a doctor on the telephone.'

Araminta spent the next two hours in the waiting room, telling herself that Thelma might want her, and hoping that she might see Doctor van Sibbelt again. But there was no sign of him. She took Thelma home presently, feeling strangely let down.

The next few days passed quietly. If Thomas had

seen Doctor van Sibbelt, he gave no sign, and Araminta could detect no change in his bullying attitude towards his wife. His impatient intolerance of her weariness was only too apparent, and he did little or nothing to curb Bertram's tiresome demands to have this or that done for him. Araminta, sending the boy sulkily to his bed long after he should have been there, found herself speculating as to what would happen when Thomas was left on his own to cope with the boy.

It was the following morning when Thelma, sitting dressing-gowned in the living room while Araminta vacuumed, collapsed. She did it so quietly that Araminta, who had her back to her, heard no sound; only when she turned round did she see Thelma sagging in an untidy heap in her chair.

It was something she had dreaded and half expected. She switched off the vacuum cleaner, laid the unconscious girl back in her chair, took an almost imperceptible pulse and flew to the telephone. It didn't occur to her to ring anyone else but Doctor van Sibbelt at the hospital, and when she heard his voice very calm in her ear, she told him what had happened without wasting words. And nor did he. His: 'I'll be with you in less than ten minutes, and see that the front door is open,' was all she needed to hear. She went back to Thelma, and was still trying to revive her when he arrived.

He said without preamble: 'I'll carry her into the bedroom,' and stooped to pick up the inanimate form while Araminta went ahead of him opening doors and turning back the bed covers, then sped back to the living room for his bag. It was only when he was busy with phial and syringe that he asked: 'How did it happen?'

She told him with concise brevity and he nodded. 'It

was to be expected. There was nothing to worry you until she collapsed?'

'No—she's been very bright for the last day or so, although very tired. I asked Thomas to mention that to the doctor.'

He bent over his patient. 'Telephone Mr Shaw and tell him to come now. When does the boy get home?'

'Not until almost four o'clock.' She was already half way to the door.

Thomas wasn't available, said a brisk voice at the other end of the line; he had given instructions that he was on no account to be disturbed.

'Tell him it concerns his wife,' said Arainta, 'and kindly look sharp about it.'

There was an annoyed gasp and the brisk voice said: 'There is no need…'

'Oh, yes, there is—this is urgent, life and death urgent.'

She cut Thomas ruthlessly short when she heard him prosily telling her not to disturb him with hysterical messages. 'You'd better come home—now—Thomas. Thelma's collapsed. The doctor's with her; she's unconscious.'

She didn't wait to hear his reply, but slammed down the receiver and darted back to the bedroom to meet Doctor van Sibbelt's steady eye. He moved away from the bed and said softly: 'A few minutes at the most, I'm afraid—she isn't responding at all.' He bent and took off Thelma's shoes and laid them neatly on the floor. Not looking at Araminta, he went on: 'This is the best way, you know. There was no chance at all.'

'Yes, I know. Is there anything I can do?'

He shook his head. 'Nothing at all.' He crossed the room and took her hands in his. 'Don't look like that.'

She said soberly: 'She's only thirty-five, you know—it's very young...' she had been going to say 'to die', but she choked on the words.

He tucked a hand under her arm and drew her back to the bed and they waited quietly side-by-side. Presently he leaned down and took Thelma's pulse, then straightened himself. 'A truly peaceful end,' he said, and added something in Dutch.

'You don't think she knew?'

'She would have known nothing.' He paused as the flat door was opened and Thomas's deliberate tread crossed the hall. He began to speak before he reached the bedroom, in a blustering, aggrieved voice: 'Araminta, what is all this? I really cannot have you sending hysterical messages...' He broke off, standing in the doorway while his rather high colour faded slowly. 'Why wasn't I told sooner?' he wanted to know.

The doctor looked at him with distaste. 'Your wife died rather less than five minutes ago,' he said evenly. 'We will leave you for a little while—we can talk presently.'

He walked to the door, sweeping Araminta with him, passed Thomas and closed the door on him. In the hall he said: 'An unpleasant man. I find it hard to remember that he is a relation of yours, Araminta.'

'So do I! He always was awful—now he's older he's much worse. What do we do next?'

'Doctor de Vos should be here at any minute, I told someone to telephone him from the hospital.' The doctor's face assumed such a ferocious expression that she drew a quick breath and decided prudently not to ask any more questions for the moment. It was fortunate that the silence which followed was quickly broken by the arrival of Doctor de Vos. He was a thin, stooping man with a harassed expression, whom Doctor van Sibbelt introduced briefly before walking him up and down the hall, while they conferred together in muttered undertones. Araminta, watching them, decided that they had forgotten her and went off to the kitchen. It would have to be coffee, she decided resignedly; the Dutch took their cups of coffee as seriously as the British took their tea, and she was in the minority. She had the percolator going and cups and saucers on a tray when she heard the bedroom door open and Thomas's voice calling her, and the moment she poked her pretty nose round the door he began irritably: 'I should like to know…'

He wasn't allowed to finish. Doctor van Sibbelt interrupted him with a suavity which barely concealed the ferociousness she had observed earlier. 'Ah, Mr Shaw, but first Doctor de Vos and I would like to know why it is that you told him that there was no need for him to call and see your wife. If you remember, I asked you to telephone him each day—something you did not do—and when he contacted you, you gave him to understand that he was not to visit as Mrs Shaw's condition was very satisfactory, and this after Miss Shaw had asked you to let Doctor de Vos know that your wife was becoming increasingly tired.'

He was standing very close to Thomas now, towering over him, showing him a bland face, although Araminta sensed his fine rage as she waited to hear what Thomas would say.

Thomas blustered again. The two doctors heard him out gravely with impassive faces and slightly raised eyebrows, and presently he realized that he was getting nowhere and fell silent, looking round him until his eyes lighted upon Araminta, which caused him to say:

'You should have told me—after all, you came here to look after Thelma. You're a nurse.'

He was interrupted once more. 'No possible blame can be laid at Miss Shaw's door,' said Doctor van Sibbelt in a cold voice, 'and you are, I imagine, aware of that. I thought that I had spoken plainly enough to you the other day, but apparently you are one of those people who knows better than everyone else.' He added with quiet authority: 'Be good enough to show me where I may sign the necessary papers.'

Araminta went silently into the bedroom and fetched his bag, and he took it from her with a brief word of thanks, then disappeared into the dinning room and sat down at the table. Doctor de Vos followed him, and so, presently, did Thomas. Araminta went back to the kitchen and took the coffee off the stove and sat down. She supposed that Thomas would expect her to do a great many things when the doctors had gone. She didn't want to do them, but she couldn't refuse him, but afterwards she would pack her bag and leave as early as she could in the morning. She would be able to return to St Katherine's after all, although perhaps she should stay for the funeral…

Her thoughts were interrupted by Doctor van Sibbelt who paused in the doorway, remote and professionally impersonal, to say that he had been given to understand that they would be going to a hotel for the night.

'We have advised Mr Shaw to make all the necessary arrangements and he has done so; everything will be attended to and there should be nothing further for you to do. The boy is to go straight to friends after school, and his father will go there presently and meet him.' He glanced at his watch. 'You'll be all right! I'm afraid I must return to the hospital.'

'I'll be fine,' she assured him sturdily, 'and thank you for coming so quickly.' She looked at him in sudden consternation. 'Heavens, I suppose I shouldn't have telephoned you, but you were the first person I thought of. You must have been taking a clinic…'

'A teaching round,' he corrected her, 'but that doesn't matter, I'm glad that…' He didn't finish what he had started to say. 'Goodbye.'

Doctor de Vos went shortly after and Thomas came into the kitchen, saying stiffly: 'I shall have to stay here until they've taken Thelma away.'

'Then we'd better have coffee, Thomas. I'll bring it into the living room.'

They drank it in almost total silence and presently when the door bell rang, Thomas went away, leaving Araminta to sit listening to the murmur of voices and the slow tread of feet in the hall. When everything was quiet again she went in search of him. He was putting things into an overnight bag and when she said at once: 'Oh, shall I look out some of Bertram's things for you? Are we going now?'

He didn't quite meet her eyes, but fussed with the lock of the bag. 'I've already packed all he needs. I shall go now, but I must ask you to stay here until five o'clock or thereabouts—the office may telephone with some urgent message for me, and you can see for yourself that I must go and break the news to Bertram.'

She agreed reluctantly. To sit in the flat alone for several hours was an uninviting prospect, but it was true that Thomas had had no time in which to make any arrangements about his work. He had shown no grief at Thelma's death, but she would have to give him the benefit of the doubt. Perhaps he was suffering from shock.

He went to the door. 'I'll telephone you from my friend's house,' he told her. 'As you've nothing to do this afternoon, you could start clearing out Thelma's things.'

She looked at him with something like horror. Even allowing for shock, he was being horribly indifferent. 'No,' she forced herself to speak quietly, 'I can't do that, Thomas, she was your wife—although listening to you, I find that hard to believe. I shall pack my own things, though, and be ready to leave tomorrow.'

He stared at her in disbelief. 'But what am I to do—and what about Bertram?'

'I came here to look after Thelma. She doesn't need me any more and you haven't liked me being here, have you? Besides, I have a job to go back to, or perhaps you'd forgotten that? You must get a housekeeper, Thomas. And as for Bertram, he can't bear the sight of me, anyway.'

'You're a hard young woman,' Thomas pronounced, but she shook her head.

'No, Thomas, I'm not, but you're a hard man, and a hypocrite as well.'

He gave her a look of dislike as he opened the door and walked away without saying goodbye.

The flat was terribly quiet. Araminta packed her things, tidied the flat, drank the coffee pot dry, sitting lonely in the kitchen, then wandered into the sitting room. She felt lost and said; she hadn't known Thelma well, but she grieved for her death, and she felt guilty too because she could find no sympathy for Thomas even though he deserved none. It would be a good thing for her to get back to St Katherine's and her work once more and put the whole sad little episode out of her mind.

The unwilling thought that she wasn't going to find it

easy to put Doctor van Sibbelt out of her mind, too, disturbed her a little and to dispel her thoughts she went to the window and looked out. The early November afternoon was already fading and a steady wind was whirling the fallen leaves into untidy spirals and forcing the people walking in the street below to lower their heads against its chilly strength. It was a pity she wouldn't see more of Amsterdam; only this modern corner of it and a brief glimpse of its older streets on their trips to and from the hospital. The nearby churches tinkled out their four o'clock carillons and Araminta went to the kitchen, made some tea, and turned on the radio. She turned on the living room lights too, as well as the hideous glass lamp hanging in the hall.

It was better with the lights on. She drank her tea slowly and when the clocks chimed the hour again, tidied the tea things away, made sure that she had all she needed packed for the night and sat down again to wait for Thomas to telephone, wondering idly which hotel they would be going to. He hadn't mentioned it, now that she came to think about it, it had been Doctor van Sibbelt… Thomas hadn't told her his friend's name either, or where he lived. As her watch ticked steadily on towards six o'clock, she began to feel uneasy, especially as she wasn't sure of the name of his office or where it was. Surely he had had ample time in which to break the news to Bertram, make arrangements for them all that night, and telephone her? He had been gone for almost four hours. On the other hand, he might have encountered all sorts of difficulties which had prevented her hearing from him.

She went through the flat, switching on lights in every room but Thelma's, and found a book which she painstakingly read until she heard the clocks strike once more. It was very dark outside now, but she had left the curtains undrawn and she wandered from window to window, peering out, wondering what to do. She could of course pick up her overnight bag and go and find herself a hotel, leaving a note for Thomas, but on the other hand, if he and Bertram were to come back to the empty flat she would feel pretty mean. Perhaps his friend's address, or even his office, would be in his study. She went along to see and found that although the door was open, everything else was locked; the only information on show was the calendar on his desk. She stood staring at it, wondering what to do. She wasn't a nervous girl, but the idea of staying alone in the flat was daunting. She could of course try one of the other flats on the floor, but she had never seen any of the occupants, and supposing they couldn't understand English? And she had no key. She spent ten minutes looking for one without success and had gone back into the hall when the door bell rang, sounding very loud in the quiet, so that she jumped with fright. It rang again almost immediately—whoever it was was very impatient. Araminta walked slowly to the door and opened it, and Doctor van Sibbelt walked in.

He stood just inside the door, immaculate and calm and reassuringly large. 'I was passing,' he observed, 'and noticed that all the lights were on. I couldn't imagine that Mr Shaw would allow such an extravagance, so I came up to see what was happening.' He lifted his dark gaze from her face and looked around him. 'You're alone?'

She had had no idea that she was going to cry. The tears trickled down her cheeks and she gave a loud sniff, quite unable to say anything. The doctor drew her close, one arm round her shoulders; it held her gently, although his voice was by no means gentle. 'Cousin Thomas hasn't been back? Do you know where he is?'

She shook her head, sniffed again and said: 'He—he was going to telephone about five o'clock. He said he had to go and fetch Bertram and I'd have to stay here in case his office telephoned.'

'And did anyone telephone?'

She shook her head again, sniffed for the third time and looked at him. 'I have no idea what to do, but I'm not usually so poor-spirited—I think I'm a little tired, and it's lonely here.'

He didn't answer but took a very white handkerchief from a pocket and offered it to her. 'I should have thought of this,' he told her, 'but no matter, it can be sorted out in no time.'

She eyed him from behind the handkerchief. 'Oh—you know where Thomas is?'

'Lord, no, my dear, nor do I intend to find out. You shall come with me.'

'Oh, but I…' She was interrupted by the ringing of the telephone. 'The telephone!' she exclaimed superfluously, and hurried to answer it.

It was Thomas. Araminta listened wide-eyed to what he had to say and then spoke herself with some spirit. 'I'll do no such thing!' she declared. 'Have you no feelings at all, Thomas? I'll not stay…'

The receiver was taken from her grasp and her companion spoke: 'Doctor van Sibbelt here—am I right in supposing that you expect Araminta to remain here alone tonight?'

She could hear Thomas's querulous voice at the other end, and when the doctor said levelly: 'I think you should take care of what you are saying, Mr Shaw,' she looked at him enquiringly and asked: 'What did he say—why do you look so angry?'

'Nothing of importance. If you have your things packed, we'll go.'

'Where?'

'To my house.'

'Oh, I can't do that!' She stood a little way from him, looking out of a window.

'Afraid of your reputation, Araminta?' She could hear the mockery in his voice.

'Well, no,' she told him, considering the question carefully. 'I was really thinking of yours.'

He chuckled. 'Good of you, but quite wasted on me, I'm afraid. I have a very old aunt living with me. Her moral standards haven't altered since the turn of the century and I imagine that she is more than capable of preserving the conventions.'

'But I still can't—I mean, foist myself upon you like this. If you would be obliging enough to take me to a small hotel, I shall be quite all right.'

'No, you won't—you will sit and brood all night. Besides, surely you know by now that I only oblige myself, never anyone else? Go and put on your coat.'

It was a relief to be told what to do, and she certainly didn't want to stay alone in the flat. How mean Thomas was… She pulled on her coat without much attention to her appearance, tied a scarf over her bright hair, caught up her handbag and gloves and pronounced herself to be ready, so that it only remained for the doctor to pick up her case, turn out the lights, usher her out of the door and shut it behind them.

They saw no one on the way down and the street

outside was deserted. Drawn up to the curb was a silver grey Jensen convertible; the doctor unlocked its door, urged her to get in, cast her case on to the back seat and got in beside her, taking up a good deal more than his fair share of space. Araminta, taken aback at the car's splendour, and still wondering if she was doing the right thing, had fallen silent, and it was left to her companion to say placidly: 'You must be hungry—I know I am. I missed my lunch.'

He turned the car and slid down the street, ready to turn into the main road beyond. 'Let's hope there's something nice for supper.'

This normal remark, made in a normal voice, restored her considerably. She relaxed against the comfort of the leather seat, too tired to think of anything much, aware at the same time that she no longer felt lost or lonely.

CHAPTER FIVE

THE CAR'S ELEGANT nose was pointed towards the city's centre, and although the traffic was heavy, Doctor van Sibbelt drove with the apparent nonchalance of a cyclist in a deserted country lane. He made no attempt to talk, so that Araminta occupied herself in looking at the lighted streets, trying to guess where they were. They left the main road presently and he swept the Jensen through a succession of narrow streets lined with old houses and intercepted by small hump-backed bridges with wrought iron railings, which spanned the dark waters of any number of canals. The houses now were rather splendid, with lights shining from their wide windows, so that she could catch a glimpse of the rooms beyond as they went past. For her the drive could have gone on for the rest of the evening, but the doctor wanted his supper and it surely couldn't be much further.

It wasn't. The doctor slowed down to cross yet another bridge where two canals met, and instead of going straight on, slid across the cobbled street and stopped before an imposing corner house.

Araminta peered out of her window at its handsome

façade and asked doubtfully: 'Do you live here? Are they flats?'

'God forbid! An ancestor of mine built it a long time ago and no one has wanted to change it since—least of all myself.'

'It's very large.'

'Have you forgotten that I intend to take a wife?' He turned to look at her, half smiling.

'You'll still rattle round like two peas in a pod,' she pointed out.

'Not for long. Just lately I have felt a strong urge to become a family man.'

She gave him a shocked look. 'That's no reason for taking a wife.' She added with some warmth: 'Poor thing!'

He laughed, but there was no mockery in the sound. 'It won't be like that—my wife will be the most important thing in my life and I shall never give her the chance to think otherwise.' He got out of the car and opened the door for her. 'Welcome to my home, Araminta.'

The great front door was opened as they reached it—by the elderly man who had been on the yacht—and Araminta exclaimed: 'Oh, how nice to see you again!' She smiled widely at him, her own troubles forgotten for the moment, feeling almost carefree. Doctor van Sibbelt had taken charge of her for the moment, and now here was another old friend. She held out a hand and he said gravely 'It is for me a great pleasure also, miss,' and then looked questioningly at the doctor.

'A long story, Jos. I'll tell you later.'

They had been standing in the vestibule and now Jos threw open the inner door to disclose a long, wide hall with a branched staircase at the far end of it. The doctor threw off his coat and flung it into a great carved chair.

'My aunt has dined, Jos? Will you ask Frone to find some food for us? we're both hungry. Miss Shaw will be staying the night, so see that someone gets a room ready for her, would you. Frone can take her up presently.'

Jos murmured and went away and Araminta said: 'He's the butler, I suppose.'

'Yes—he's also a family friend of long standing. He taught me to swim and sail and skate—we still sail together.'

'He's nice…'

The doctor smiled down at her. 'Indeed he is, and I'd trust him with my life.'

She smiled back rather shyly. 'I expect he feels the same about you.'

'I like to think so. Let me have that coat—someone will take you up to your room presently, but come and meet Tante Maybella first.'

Araminta stared about her unashamedly. The hall was very imposing with its marble floor and silk rugs and lighted by an enormous chandelier and a number of wall sconces, set between a collection of large and somewhat gloomy portraits. She would have liked the opportunity to have examined them at her leisure as she allowed herself to be led across the hall, through a double-arched doorway, into a room not less imposing but having a pleasantly homely air about it, partly due to the cheerful fire burning in the wide hearth and the very ordinary tabby cat spread out before it. There was a dog too, a long-haired Alsatian, who advanced to greet them with welcoming barks and an obvious desire to put his front paws on their shoulders and look into their faces. The doctor fended him off with a cheerful: 'Manners, Rikki!' and crossed the room with Araminta held firmly by the arm.

The old lady sitting in the small upright chair by the fire was very small and frail, and this was emphasized by the black silk gown she wore and the quantity of gold chains which hung round her high frilled collar. She smiled at them as they stopped before her and said something to the doctor in a high, tinkling voice. Araminta could understand none of it, although she was very conscious of a pair of sharp blue eyes studying her as the old lady talked. She had the uneasy feeling that she wasn't welcome, but it must have been imagination, for when the doctor introduced her—in English, to her relief—his aunt smiled charmingly.

'You must tell me all about yourself,' she cried in an English as good as her nephew. 'I'm a lonely old woman, you see—if it weren't for Crispin's kindness I should be living quite by myself.'

The doctor laughed gently. 'You naughty old thing,' he chided her, 'you know as well as I do that you have a perfectly good home of your own—two, in fact, and you won't live in either of them. Besides, what should I do without you? But you shall have your gossip with Araminta presently, but first she wants to go to her room and tidy herself for supper.'

'You are staying the night?' The old lady sounded apprehensive.

Araminta smiled at her. 'The doctor kindly brought me here, because I had nowhere to go…' She was interrupted by the entrance of a large, stout woman, very neatly dressed, who spoke to the doctor and then nodded and smiled at her.

'This is Frone, Jos's wife—she will take you upstairs. She can't speak a word of English, but I have no doubt you will be able to understand each other.'

Araminta, with Frone beside her, wished once more that she could be allowed the leisure to look at everything as they went through the hall and up the stairs to a wide corridor. The room she was shown into was half way down it, a fair-sized, lofty apartment, deliciously warm and furnished with delicate Regency pieces and a great deal of pastel chintz. Her case was already there, unpacked; moreover there was a small bathroom leading from it, with everything in it that a girl could wish for. Araminta inspected it with a delighted eye. It was a charming room; she pictured it occupied by the daughter of the house and sighed without knowing it as she attended to the business of doing her face and hair.

They had drinks when she went down to the drawing room again, and then left the old lady in her chair while they traversed the hall once more to enter a small, softly lighted room with a round table at its centre, laid with a white cloth, sparkling glass and gleaming silver. Araminta had supposed that supper would be a simple meal of soup and perhaps an omelette, but she couldn't have been more mistaken. There was soup, certainly—french onion soup, served in brown earthenware pipkins, and lavishly sprinkled with cheese, but that was followed by poached turbot and lobster sauce, accompanied by a salad. There was a Charlotte Russe to follow these dainties, and all of them helped along nicely by the hock which the doctor poured for them both, so that Araminta's pale face got back some of the healthy pink it had lost.

All the while they ate, the doctor kept up a smooth flow of talk about nothing in particular, so that presently she began to forget her unhappy day, and by the time they went back to the drawing room for coffee with old Mevrouw van Sibbelt, she was nicely relaxed and had no difficulty in answering that lady's numerous questions for the next hour or so, and when the old lady went to bed, she got to her feet too, with the intention of doing the same thing. But her host had other ideas. He ushered his aged relative to the door, kissed her cheek, then closed it firmly before Araminta was anywhere near it. 'A little talk?' he suggested. 'I know you're tired and you've had a wretched day, but it's barely ten o'clock—I think we should make a few arrangements for tomorrow, don't you? You said you wished to go back to England—would you like me to get you a seat on a morning flight?'

He sounded a little remote and disinterested, but then, Araminta told herself, why should he be anything else? He had been kind and helpful, but probably he would be glad to see the back of her. He had gone to sit by the fire again, with Rikki beside him, and it struck her with the most unexpected suddenness that it would be nothing short of happiness to sit opposite him for the rest of her life. He would probably be a difficult husband, but she saw no reason why she couldn't manage him. She remembered with a pang of pure sorrow that he had already told her that he had plans to marry…

'You're wearing a sad look. Why?' he asked.

She had no intention of telling him, instead she said briskly: 'I don't think I had better go home—not just yet. I can't, you know. I can't stand Thomas—or Bertram—but they'll need someone for a day or two, just until the funeral is over and he can find a housekeeper. Father and Aunt Martha would expect me to do that.'

He smiled faintly. 'I expected you to do that too, Araminta. I'll take you back in the morning, if you like,

I don't need to be at the hospital until nine o'clock—will that be too early for you? Have you a key?'

She shook her head. 'No, but surely Thomas will be there? He said something about someone coming in the morning.'

'We'll go and see, and if there is no one there, I'll bring you back here.'

'Thank you, but I shall be quite all right.'

He didn't dispute this, only smiled again. 'Would you like to telephone your father?' he asked.

'Oh, yes, please!'

'And the hospital?'

Araminta hesitated. St Katherine's was the last place she wanted to see; once she got back there, the doctor would be someone to forget about as quickly as possible, and she didn't want to do that, not yet. While she stayed in Amsterdam she had a chance of seeing something of him, and while she knew it was a futile thing to do, she couldn't bring herself to do anything else. 'I had three weeks' unpaid leave,' she told him a little breathlessly.

'So you did,' he agreed gravely. 'Will Thomas be glad to see you?'

'No, but I think he'll be glad to have someone to cook and look after the flat for a day or two.'

'He might want you to stay indefinitely.'

She shook her head. 'Oh, no, he wouldn't; he'd have to pay me a salary, and that would seem like a waste of money to him—paying a cousin.'

Her companion stretched his long legs and lounged back in his chair. 'You're a very pretty girl,' he observed matter-of-factly, 'hasn't anyone wanted to marry you?'

She flushed a little but answered with a total lack of conceit: 'Oh, yes.'

'And you've always said no?'

She nodded, looking away from him. How surprised he would be if she told him that if he cared to ask her she would say yes at once. He didn't, of course, but went on half mockingly: 'Don't tell me that you're a dedicated nurse?'

'Certainly not. I like nursing very much and I have to earn my living.' She didn't want to talk about it any more; she cast around for a suitable topic of conversation and came up with: 'Is there a shortage of nurses in Holland?'

There was a spark of amusement in his eyes, but he followed her cue and they discussed nursing and hospitals and the newest theatre equipment until Araminta finally said good night and escaped to bed. Any other girl, she thought dispiritedly, would have turned an hour of the doctor's company to her own advantage. All she had done was to illustrate to him what a dull creature she was, making stilted conversation about her work. He had probably been bored stiff. It only surprised her that he hadn't said so; he hadn't struck her as a man to suffer fools gladly.

Despite her troubled thoughts she fell asleep in her comfortable bed at once and didn't wake until she was roused by a strapping girl with pink cheeks and blue eyes, bearing her morning tea. As soon as the girl had gone, Araminta got out of bed and padded across the thick carpet to peer out of the window. It was another grey day, with rain dripping from the rooftops and the early morning traffic making its way through wet streets. It matched her mood; Thomas and Bertram loomed large on her horizon, and larger still was the thought that after the doctor had deposited her at her cousin's flat in an hour or two's time, she might not see him again.

But mooning around being sorry for herself would do no good. She bathed and dressed and went downstairs, to find her host in the hall going through his post. The sight of him sent her heart thudding, but despite that she achieved a good morning in an ordinary enough voice as she bent to pat Rikki's great head.

The doctor made a cheerful good morning in reply, adding: 'My name's Crispin. Tante Maybella doesn't come down to breakfast, so you must excuse her, and I, I regret to say, have formed the bad habit of reading my letters while I eat—that's what comes of being a bachelor. You won't mind?' He smiled charmingly. 'I have so little time.'

'I don't mind at all,' she declared with earnest mendacity. 'I have a great deal to think about, anyway.'

So breakfast was an almost silent meal, relieved only by Jos's solemn greeting and their own polite exchanges concerning more coffee, more toast and the expression of mutual agreement over the pleasure of hot croissants for breakfast. And the drive to Thomas's flat was almost as silent. The doctor looked thoughtful, as he drove and Araminta, imagining him to be concentrating upon the day's work ahead of him, held her tongue. She was a little pale as they went up the stairs together, though, for she had just realised that she had made no plans in the event of no one being home.

But someone was there. In answer to the doctor's firm knock, and for good measure, his finger on the bell, Bertram opened the door.

He grinned slyly at Araminta, and without bothering to say hullo declared: 'Father said you'd be back. He told me to wait until you came—he's gone to work. There's a list of things he wants you to do on the dining room table.'

His two listeners observed him with astonishment, Araminta burning with rage at the cool assumption that she would go back and cope. Instructions, indeed! She was about to make herself very plain on that point when Bertram remarked carelessly: 'I'm going to my friend's now. I don't have to go to school—not till the funeral's over.' He smirked. 'Three days' holiday!'

Araminta's hand itched to box his ears. 'Why, you horrid, unnatural…' and was drowned in the subdued thunder of the doctor's voice.

'Get inside, boy! You'll stay here until you have done everything Araminta wishes you to do and go only when she says so.' He looked and sounded so fierce that the boy backed away, staring at him. 'And be sure,' continued the doctor, 'that I shall know if you do otherwise. Be good enough to carry your cousin's bag to her room.'

It was Bertram's turn to look amazed. He picked up the case meekly enough, though, and took it along to Araminta's room. Then Doctor van Sibbelt said: 'I must go, I'm afraid—you know where I am if you want me.' He bent and kissed her swiftly and started on his way down the stairs, not looking back once.

Araminta, once she had stifled the urge to run after the doctor, plunged into the numerous tasks Thomas had seen fit to leave her, but she took care to see that Bertram helped her. He did it ungraciously, but at least he did the small jobs she gave him to do while she started on the pile of washing in the little laundry room off the kitchen. Poor Thelma had obviously got very behind with the laundry. Araminta had done everything she could lay her hands on when she had first arrived, but this lot must have been hidden away somewhere. She got the first batch out on the line on the kitchen balcony and went to look in the fridge. There was food enough. She put the coffee on and went back to her washing. Once that was out of the way she would have time to unpack her things. The flat didn't look too bad—true, Thomas had left the breakfast things on the table, but she prevailed upon Bertram to clear them away.

The washing out of the way, she poured coffee for them both and sat down to drink it. Bertram was sulking. She suspected that he had had things very much his own way while Thelma had been ill, and looking at him now, she could see no sign of grief on his face.

'Will you mind having a housekeeper here?' she asked him.

He shrugged. 'What do I care who comes? Anyway, Father says you'll stay.'

Her fine eyes sparkled. 'Did he now? But you see, Bertram, I'm not going to stay, only until the funeral.'

'I'm not going!' he told her loudly.

'Well, I hardly thought you would,' she agreed, and added gently: 'Will you miss your mother very much, Bertram?'

'Miss her? No—she was always ill. Father says she didn't think about us, only thought about herself.'

Araminta felt the tears prick her eyelids. 'That's not true! Your mother thought about you both—she was ill, and it seems to me that neither of you cared.' And when he shrugged: 'You'd better go to your friend's house, Bertram.'

She got up and walked out of the kitchen, anxious to be free of his company. It was better when he had gone. She dusted and mopped and got herself some lunch which she didn't eat after all, then went to the kitchen to get the supper ready. Thomas would be home, presumably about six. There were pork chops in the fridge and a carton of custard. If she got the vegetables done now she would have the afternoon to herself. But that wasn't very satisfactory, as it turned out, for she sat doing nothing, tired from all the washing, allowing her mind to wander. Which it did, but always back to Crispin. Such a waste of time, she told herself crossly, and went to see if the clothes were dry.

She had supper almost ready when Thomas came in. He had Bertram with him and it was obvious that the boy had been telling tales, for his father, greeting him with his usual pomposity, added: 'I'm told that you made Bertram do a great many chores this morning—I don't care for your attitude towards him, Araminta.'

'Well, you expect me to do a great many chores, don't you, Thomas? And I don't care for your attitude towards me, either.' Araminta's pretty face went pink. 'And if you think I came back because I wanted to,' she snapped, 'you're very much mistaken. I came back because of Thelma.'

He had the grace to look uncomfortable, but only for a moment. 'I shall work for half an hour in my study,' he announced, 'and supper promptly at seven o'clock.' He gave her a frowning glance. 'I've had a busy day, arranging for the funeral and so on, and of course my normal work must be done at all costs.'

She wished he wouldn't talk as though the world would crumble unless he did a day's work in the office. She muttered something and went back to the kitchen.

At five to the hour the front door bell rang, and at its second peal, knowing that no one would answer it unless she did, Araminta went, not in the best of tempers, to open it. Crispin was leaning against the wall outside.

'You took your time,' he observed. 'You look as though you've been slaving over a hot stove, too.'

'Well, I have,' she told him testily, aware that the apron she had put on did nothing for her at all and that her hair was no longer neat. She had been thinking about him all day, and now that he was here, he was making unkind remarks! Self-pity tied itself in a knot in her throat as she glared at him, to be instantly disarmed by his placid:

'Well, it suits you—there's nothing like an apron to give a girl that little extra something.'

She laughed then and he said cheerfully: 'That's better! Now do take it off, there's a dear girl, and put on a coat. We're going out to dinner.'

'But the chops—' she told him worriedly.

He peered past her into the gloomy hall. 'Anyone home? Yes? Surely they don't need your help in dishing them up and eating them?' He edged past her, took the door handle out of her hand and closed the door behind him, and said: 'Ten minutes?'

Her self-pity and bad temper had disappeared. She nodded happily and skipped down the hall to her room, she had the door open when Thomas came out of his study. 'Who…?' he began, and stopped as his eyes fell on the doctor, who wished him good evening in a frosty voice and added:

'I'm taking Araminta out to dinner.' Thomas made a gobbling noise and the doctor walked past him to where Araminta was still standing, pushed her gently into the room and closed the door. 'You have no objection?' he wanted to know silkily.

'Going out to dinner and Thelma dead barely a day?' said Thomas in a righteous voice.

Doctor van Sibbelt smiled nastily, his dark face quite menacing. 'Will you be going without your dinner?' he asked. 'I should be careful what you say, Mr Shaw.' His voice was as nasty as his smile, so that Thomas subsided, his face very red, and muttering that he supposed he would have to see to the supper himself, went loftily to the kitchen.

Araminta, happily unaware of this brief conversation, whipped out of her slacks and sweater and took a doubtful look at her scanty wardrobe. She had worn the suit yesterday, which left her with the jersey dress and her winter coat. She changed rapidly, did her face, put up her golden hair, snatched up handbag and gloves and went back into the hall, where she found the doctor standing gazing at nothing. But his abstracted air left him when he saw her. 'Do you still have a key?' he asked.

She nodded. 'Thomas left me one this morning—so that I could do the shopping.' She went along to the kitchen to say good night to Thomas and found him dishing up the chops. He threw her a sulky look.

'You're a poor housekeeper,' he observed in a patronising tone which led her to suggest that he got himself a good one at the earliest possible moment. 'I shall advertise tomorrow,' he assured her. 'After a year of Thelma's slapdash ways and now you...a man needs to be looked after.'

Araminta didn't trust herself to reply, for her pent-up emotions were almost choking her, so that when she rejoined the doctor he observed mildly: 'You've had your feathers ruffled again, I see. We had better go quickly before I do your cousin some injury.'

On the stairs she said uncertainly: 'I feel mean—I ought to feel sorry for Thomas and Bertram…'

Crispin caught her by the arm so that she was forced to stand still and look at him. 'Was he sorry for his wife?' he demanded. 'I don't believe in an eye for an eye, but can't you see that pity is quite wasted on a man like that?' He kept his hand on her arm and hurried her down the rest of the stairs and out to where the Jensen was parked.

He took her to Dikker and Thijs in the Leidsestraat, where they were shown to a discreet corner table. Araminta couldn't help but notice that her companion was well-known at the restaurant, and she found herself speculating as to who he brought there. The sharp prick of jealousy confused her so much that he had to ask her twice what she would like to drink.

Thinking about it later, she wasn't quite sure what she had had to eat, only that everything tasted delicious, served in elegant peace and quiet, and that her companion had been an amusing and thoughtful host. There were so many facets to his character; the ill-tempered yachtsman, the suave doctor, and now the perfect host. She found herself wondering which was the real Crispin. Not that it mattered, she loved him whatever he chose to be.

He hadn't taken her back to the flat after their leisurely meal, but had driven to his home, where Jos had quite obviously been glad to see her, and just as obviously Tante Maybella hadn't. The old lady had had friends to dinner, but they had been gone some time before Araminta and the doctor returned, and she complained in her high, sweet little voice that she had been lonely and had given Araminta a look which gave her plainly to understand that she had been the cause of it. Which was probably why she remained in the drawing room talking animatedly until Crispin had suggested that it was long past her usual bedtime, when she observed gently: 'But, my dears, I have been waiting up so that I might wish Araminta good-bye.' Which seemed such a strong hint to Araminta that she said at once that she hadn't realised that it was so late and got up to go.

Crispin had said nothing at all, only smiled faintly and the hope that he would protest died almost before she was aware of it. Araminta said her goodbyes nicely, quite understanding that the old lady was jealous of her, although she wasn't sure why—surely Mevrouw van Sibbelt wasn't jealous of all the doctor's friends? and surely he entertained them when he chose? After all, it was his house.

He had driven her back to the flat without any attempt to dally on the way, and she wished him good night and thanked him quickly as he drew up outside the entrance. The evening, she felt, hadn't been all that satisfactory. Dinner had been delightful, she had relaxed and enjoyed every minute of it, but sitting between him and his aged aunt in his magnificent drawing room hadn't been very successful. Perhaps she wasn't cut out for the restrained opulence in which he lived.

She got out of the car and found that he had got out too, to walk upstairs with her, not hurrying at all, talking of their evening just as though it had been a smash hit. Outside Thomas's door he put his hands on her shoulders and said: 'You found Tante Maybella hard going, didn't you? Have patience with her, dear girl. She can't help but love you in time, but she has to get used to you—the idea of you.'

He caught her close and kissed her, a gentle, tender kiss, and then had taken the key from her hand and opened the door for her. 'Good night, dear Araminta!' She had closed the door on her own whispered good night.

She had ample time to think about it all the next day, once she had got Thomas off to the office and Bertram away to his friend's house. In the light of a cold November day it seemed clear to her that she was allowing her own feelings to run away with her. Just because she was in love with Crispin there was no good reason for supposing that he was in love with her—on the contrary, he was being kind, in the same way as he would be kind to a lost puppy who had thrown itself on his mercy, or an old lady who had lost her purse. For he was a kind man, despite his mocking manner upon occasion and his black looks. She allowed her thoughts to become daydreams while she did the housework.

Crispin had said nothing about seeing her again. There was a chicken in the fridge, so she prepared it for the evening meal, peeled potatoes, opened a can of peas and found another carton of custard, chocolate this time. An uninspired meal, but shopping was still something of a closed book to her and Thomas hadn't even bothered to tell her where the nearest food shops were. She filled in the afternoon with the ironing, put the chicken in the oven and went to lay the table. One more day, she promised herself, and she would be able to go home with an easy conscience; Thomas would just have to find himself a housekeeper. When he got home she would have a talk with him and ask at the same time what arrangements had been made for the following day. The funeral was to be in the morning, and as Thelma had no relatives and very few friends, presumably no one would come back to the flat.

Araminta went to baste the bird and then answer the telephone. It was Crispin. 'I'll be round about eight o'clock,' he told her, for all the world as though he had already told her he would be coming. 'We'll have dinner at home, shall we?' he asked her. 'I'm going to be held up this evening, but I won't be later than that.'

'I've a chicken in the oven,' Araminta told him.

'What a busy little housewife you are! Thomas and Bertram will enjoy it. *Tot ziens*.'

Thomas wasn't too pleased when she told him, but he had really nothing to complain about, for the meal was ready for him to eat, and what was more, there was ample time for her to wash up before she went to get ready. She would have had even more time if one or other of them had helped her, but all the same, she was ready and waiting when the doctor arrived. They left the flat together after the most casual of greetings on Crispin's part, and Araminta kept quiet during their brief drive, for he looked tired and preoccupied, so much so that before they entered the house she asked hastily: 'You are sure you want me to come? I'll quite understand...you've been busy, haven't you? I daresay all you want to do is sit down by the fire with a drink and the papers.'

'I'll settle for you instead of the papers,' he said, half laughing. 'I've had a heavy day, but I would rather be with you than with anyone else, Araminta.' He opened the door and ushered her inside. 'You seem to have grown on me.'

Such an awkward observation to answer, she decided, and said nothing at all, concluding that he wasn't expecting one. Jos, advancing upon them from the back of the hall, took his master's coat, wished them both a good evening, indicated that Araminta might wish to go upstairs to tidy herself, and retired again.

'Do you really need to go upstairs?' asked the doctor. 'You look perfectly all right to me. There's a mirror if you want to look at your face—women usually do.'

'Just for that, I shan't look,' said Araminta crisply, and was whirled round to be kissed swiftly.

'Such a lovely girl,' declared Crispin thoughtfully. 'She never minces her words, cooks chickens to a turn, knows what to do when a bomb goes off, and always looks dishy. I shall have to do something about it.'

Araminta longed to ask what, but didn't. For one thing she felt sure that he was teasing her, and as she couldn't think of anything gay or clever to say, it seemed wise to remain silent. She smiled rather uncertainly at him and watched his features become placid again.

'Drinks,' he suggested cheerfully, and led the way to the drawing room where Tante Maybella was awaiting them.

The old lady greeted her warmly, so that Araminta decided that she had been quite mistaken on the previous evening and enjoyed her dinner very much in consequence, with Mevrouw van Sibbelt regaling her companions with tales of her youth and the people she had known. Her gaiety had tired her, though, for shortly after they returned to the drawing room, she declared that she would go to bed and wished Araminta as warm a good night as her welcome had been before trotting off with Crispin to escort her to the stairs.

He was back in a very short time to ask her: 'Would you like to see something of the house? There are some rather nice pictures and some silver and porcelain.'

They were housed in the library, a vast apartment, its walls lined with books, its polished floor covered with a Persian carpet. There were comfortable chairs arranged in groups round mahogany tables, and a bright fire burning below the magnificently carved chimney piece. They went slowly from one display cabinet to the next, while the doctor explained about Tiger ware, of which he had several specimens, and then pointed out the beauties of the *nef* which took pride of place in his collection—it was a salt, made in the shape of a ship, and was, he declared, early sixteenth century. Araminta admired it dutifully, although she very much preferred a George the Second shell pattern sugar box, which, while neither so old nor so rare, she considered to be a great deal prettier.

The glass was exquisite, too, housed in a great bow-fronted cabinet lined with blue velvet, and she pored long minutes over a goblet by Verzelini before enquiring how it came into the doctor's hands. 'Elizabethan, isn't it?' she essayed. 'Were the English and Dutch friendly then?'

'On and off. One of my ancestors married an Englishwoman and that was part of her dowry. One of the daughters of the marriage married an Englishman in her turn and their son gave my family the diamond-pinched *roemer*, just behind the goblet. Personally, I like the Beilby goblets—and there's that truly priceless *doppelpokal* on the top shelf. I feel guilty every time I see it because I dislike it so much.'

Araminta laughed. 'You ought to be bloated with the pride of possession,' she told him as they crossed the room to a smaller cabinet housing a collection of dainty china—a hand-painted tea-set, violets on the thinnest of porcelain. Araminta exclaimed: 'I like this best of all…'

'My father gave it to my mother when they were first

married. He had it specially made for her because she loved violets. I like it too.' He gave her a brief glance. 'She died when I was thirty, almost ten years ago, and my father died two years before her; he was a good deal older. They were devoted.'

'Have you any brothers or sisters?'

'Oh, yes. A young brother in Canada and two sisters, both married. One lives in Groningen, the other travels a good deal; her husband builds bridges.' He grinned suddenly. 'All I have left is Tante Maybella.'

'Oh, you really must do something about it,' cried Araminta, quite carried away by pity for his loneliness and not stopping to think what she was saying.

Crispin had come to stand very close to her and now he took her hands in his and asked unexpectedly: When do you return to St Katherine's?'

She was quite unable to answer immediately; surprise had her tongue, and a half-felt disappointment, too. She stared up at him, her dark blue eyes wide. The day after tomorrow. It's—it's the funeral tomorrow morning, you know, and I told Thomas I wouldn't stay any longer.'

His hands moved a little on hers, holding them closer. 'When you get back, will you resign?'

Shock took her breath. 'Resign? Whatever for? I haven't another job.'

He ignored that. 'And during that time—before you leave—will you think of me?'

Her eyes hadn't left his face. 'Yes.'

'Good—you see, I want to be very sure, Araminta, you've seen me at my best and almost at my worst. I'm not an easy man, you know that, but I'm prepared to wait—you are young and not very worldly.' He smiled, and when she would have spoken: 'No, don't say anything, dear girl, not now.' He bent to kiss her. 'I'll take you back to the flat now.'

CHAPTER SIX

ARAMINTA, NATURALLY ENOUGH, spent a great deal of the night deep in thought, a circumstance hardly likely to improve her day, which, when it came, was far worse than anything she could have imagined. Bertram had been fetched after breakfast, to spend yet another day at his friend's home, and that had left Thomas and herself. She had cleared up while he gloomed round the flat, making no effort to help her, and it wasn't until she was almost finished that he disclosed the fact that a dozen or so people would be coming back after the funeral.

Araminta paused in her carpet sweeping. 'Thomas, you never said a word! Will they want coffee and sandwiches? There's no time…'

'Naturally I shall offer my friends refreshment,' he told her. 'I've arranged for sandwiches to be sent in, all that's required of you is to make and serve the coffee.'

He was hateful! She felt her temper rising and tried to subdue it so that she could answer him in a normal voice. 'I'll do my best—and Thomas, I've had no chance to tell you, but you must have guessed, anyway. I'm going back to St Katherine's tomorrow—an early morning flight.' That wasn't quite true, but he might argue with her unless she was quite definite. She would have to make arrangements later on; she didn't want to stay any longer now, she had done all she could, and a thankless task it had been, too. She listened, not very attentively, to his prosy voice going on and on about her lack of loyalty, her selfishness and the impossibility of coping with the flat, the shopping, Bertram and above all, his work. When he paused for breath she observed sensibly: 'Well, Thomas, you've had two or three days in which to find a housekeeper, and surely your friends will rally round—they always do, you know.'

'Naturally they will,' he said stiffly, 'but I'm more than surprised that you should bring up the subject of leaving today of all days.'

She turned to face him, very pink. 'But today isn't any different from any other for you, is it? You aren't grieved about Thelma, are you, so why pretend?'

She had gone to the kitchen and started banging the cups and saucers on to the trays, longing for the day to be over.

Four hours later, listening to the church bells ringing out one o'clock, she realised that there was still a lot of the day left. Thomas's friends had come back with them, and sat around drinking the coffee she handed round, and the sandwiches—not nearly enough—had all been eaten up so that she had had to go to the kitchen and cut more. They had talked in loud, high voices, commiserating with Thomas while they cast accusing looks at Araminta. Thomas had obviously got them all on his side—and no one mentioned Thelma. Araminta disappeared into the kitchen as soon as she could and began on the piles of crockery. She had no wish to wash up, but it would be something to do, and it would be better to clean the cups and saucers than throw them around the kitchen, an action which would have suited her mood exactly. She was half was through her task when the door bell rang; no one would hear it in the living room, judging from the hubbub of talk going on there, so she wiped her hands down the front of her apron and went to see who it was.

Crispin slid his bulk round the door, and the mere sight of him sent such a wave of happiness through her that she had much ado not to clasp her soapy hands round his neck.

He closed the door gently behind him and surveyed her slowly before observing: 'You look like Cinderella—why are you covered in an apron?'

'I'm washing up—Thomas's friends came back here…' she choked suddenly and felt his arm on her shoulder.

'Go and take that thing off and put on a coat and something on your head, for it's cold—we're going out.'

'Out?' she repeated foolishly. 'What about the hospital—your patients—it's only a little past one o'clock…'

'What a girl you are for keeping my nose to the grindstone! Occasionally I give myself a half day—I'm having one now. Go and get your coat.'

'Thomas?'

He smiled, looking all at once forbidding and quite frighteningly remote. 'Leave Thomas to me,' he advised her blandly.

Going downstairs with him five minutes later she asked apprehensively: 'Was he angry?'

'So-so, my dear, so-so. At what time do you leave tomorrow?'

She stopped on the landing the better to explain. 'Though it doesn't really matter, just as long as I can get away from here early. There must be dozens of flights—anyway, there are boats too,' she added vaguely.

'Leave it to me. I'll telephone presently and get you a morning flight, if that's what you want. Have you telephoned the hospital?'

Araminta's lovely eyes grew round. 'Oh, no, I quite forgot—there's still time?'

'Of course there is, goose. Have you enough money?'

It seemed the most natural thing in the world that he should ask her that, so she answered him matter-of-factly: 'Yes, thank you. I took a single ticket when I came because I didn't know how long I'd be here.'

Crispin took her arm and they went out into the bleak afternoon and crossed the pavement to where a Rolls-Royce Carmargue was parked. When the doctor unlocked its door and invited her to enter, she hesitated. 'But where's the Jensen?' she wanted to know.

He went round the beautiful bonnet and got in beside her. 'At home. When I take a long trip I use this one.' He turned to smile at her. 'I hope it makes up for the *kaas broodje*.'

'I've never been in a Rolls before,' she confided, and then remembered what he had just said. 'You were saying a long trip…'

'Not so very long; to the sea to blow some colour into that white face of yours and then up to Friesland and back through the Veluwe—that's one of the prettiest parts of Holland, although it will be dark long before we get there—all the same, you'll see a little of the country.'

'How lovely' Her eyes sparkled. 'The day's been beastly, and now it's marvellous!'

She didn't see the gleam in his eyes as he allowed the Rolls to slide into the traffic. They didn't talk much as he drove through the city and out of it again on to the motorway to den Haag. Here there was room and to spare on the broad road even though the traffic was heavy. The car shot forward into a silent speed and the doctor asked abruptly: 'Do you want to talk about this morning? It will help, you know.'

Araminta drew a deep breath. 'Oh, may I? Just—just to get it off my chest.'

'Quite—talk on, my dear.'

She wasn't his dear—at least she didn't think so. He liked her, it had been wonderful to discover that, but it was just possible that he wanted her to go away so that he could discover if he did more than like her. Falling in love, she reflected, must come in a number of ways. It had hit her on the head; a great thump from which she was still recovering, but perhaps for some people it was a slow process and they weren't quite sure about it for a considerable time.

'I'm listening,' said Crispin patiently, and she abandoned her thoughts and plunged into an account of the morning. She paused a good deal and started any number of sentences she never finished, but she knew that she had her companion's attention. She petered out finally and he said in a kind voice: 'That's better, isn't it? We're just coming into den Haag; we'll go on to Scheveningen and take a quick walk by the sea, that should blow the last unhappy thoughts from your head.'

He began to point out the places which he thought might interest her as they edged their way through the crowded streets and then picked up speed again for the last mile or two to the coast.

It was hardly the day for a walk. There was a howling gale blowing into their faces and great grey clouds sweeping in from the sea to smother the colourless sky above them. Araminta, with the doctor's arm through hers, stepped out briskly into the teeth of the wind, her gorgeous hair streaming from beneath her scarf, her eyes watering, and with barely enough breath to breathe with, let alone talk. But it made her feel wonderful, and when they turned back, bowling along now at a fine pace, she cried: 'This is great!'

Crispin came to a halt and turned her round to look at her. 'Pink cheeks,' he observed, 'and a pink nose too.' He bent to kiss it lightly and walked on, sweeping her along with him.

'Tea?' he suggested when they reached the car.

She could think of nothing nicer, and then clapped her hand to her head. 'But I can't; not like this—my hair's all over the place.'

'Put it back where it belongs then.' He sat patiently, holding pins and comb and anything else she thrust at him, assuring her finally that she looked very nice as she tied her scarf back on.

They had tea at Maison Krul, in a delightful atmosphere redolent of Queen Victoria. It was still early in the afternoon and there were few customers. Araminta, eating some of the richest cakes she had ever seen in her life, suspected that Crispin had brought her there because it was exactly the kind of teashop a girl would like, a thought which triggered off another, not so pleasant idea. Perhaps he was in the habit of bringing all his girl-friends here. She frowned so fiercely that he wanted to know what ailed her. 'Nothing,' she declared hastily, and added ingenuously: 'What do you usually do when you have a free afternoon?'

She had asked for it—that mocking little smile, that pleasantly snubbing voice: 'Why, Araminta, exactly what I am doing now, of course, taking the prettiest girl I know out to tea.'

She bent her head over her plate, feeling a fool. And yet he had hinted at all kinds of things—or hadn't he? Had she been indulging in wishful thinking? After a moment she said in a cold voice: 'I'm sure they must enjoy that very much.'

Crispin seemed bent on needling her. 'I enjoy it too.' He grinned at her across the little round table. 'Have another of these cakes.'

'No, thank you.' She wondered how many other girls he had said just those words to, and as though he had read her thoughts, he said quietly—and there was no mockery now: 'You're not just a pretty girl I'm taking out to tea, Araminta.'

On the road once more they travelled fast, bypassing Leiden, which, the doctor pointed out, needed several days in order to explore it properly, and then racing up the motorway to Alkmaar, to turn off across the rather bare countryside along the road leading to the Afsluitdijk. The afternoon was clearer now, with a watery sun getting low in the sky, and it was still possible to see something of the country around them. The doctor kept up a running commentary and Araminta, wishing to miss nothing, peered from side to side, asking endless questions, which he answered with remarkable patience.

They seemed to flash across the Afsluitdijk and once on the mainland of Friesland, they skirted Harlingen to turn off on to a minor road so that she might see something of Franeker and its splendid town hall.

Leeuwarden, when they reached it soon after, was already brightly lighted, its streets bustling with shoppers, for it was getting dark now, but the Rolls' powerful headlamps lighted the road ahead of them as they took the road south, through Heereveen and Steenwijk and Meppel and on to Deventer. Araminta couldn't see much now, but the soundless speed of the car was very soothing; she could have gone on for ever and she had lost count of the time. It was only when Crispin observed: 'We're going to have a meal soon, just a few miles the other side of Amersfoort,' that she realised how hungry she was.

They left the motorway at Amersfoort and took a country road to Scherpenzeel, a large village where Crispin parked the car outside an old country inn with which Araminta instantly fell in love. The food matched its attractive appearance, too; she ate with a good appetite, her cheeks still nicely pink, her eyes sparkling. They didn't hurry over their meal; the restaurant was almost empty and no one seemed impatient for them to go. Araminta, her tongue loosened by the warmth and good food, had quite a lot to say, more than she had intended perhaps, led gently on by her companion's quiet comments and questions. She forgot the time completely, and it wasn't until they were in the car again, driving the last thirty odd miles back to Amsterdam that she looked at the clock and exclaimed in a bemused voice: 'It's after nine o'clock! I had no idea—we must have driven miles…'

He flashed her a smile. 'About three hundred miles.'

'It seemed… I've forgotten this morning,' she confessed.

'That is what I hoped.'

'I haven't done anything about my seat on the plane—it's too late.'

'I think not. We'll call in at the house and telephone Schiphol.'

She relaxed again. It was lovely to be taken care of, not to have to make plans and worry about times and flights and cooking meals. She closed her eyes in a happy daze and presently her tired head slid sideways on to Crispin's shoulder.

He wakened her gently when they reached the house, and she apologised, feeling foolish, until he told her: 'Your head fitted very nicely into my shoulder—I enjoyed the experience.' He smiled at her and her heart jumped a little. It was a good thing that Jos opened the door then and they went inside, into the softly lighted hall and thence to the cosy little room at the back of the house, where Araminta was told to sit down while the doctor telephoned. Jos appeared seconds later with coffee, and Crispin broke off his conversation to ask her to pour out, something she did very carefully from the beautiful silver coffee pot. She handed him a fragile porcelain cup and said: 'I ought to be at the flat—it's late.'

He only smiled as he sat down opposite her. 'I've booked a seat for you on the midday flight tomorrow, I have to be at the hospital, but Jos will call for you and drive you to Schiphol.' And when she protested. 'No, Araminta, don't argue.'

She stammered a little. 'It's very kind of you,' she began awkwardly.

'There's something more than kindness between us,' he told her quietly.

Her cup rattled in the saucer as she set it down, and she said quickly for something to say: 'It will be awfully strange working in hospital again—it seems like another life.'

'But not for long. I'll make no promises about seeing you again, Araminta, because it isn't easy for me to make plans and keep to them. You understand that?'

'Yes, of course.' She smiled brightly, but her mouth had gone dry. Did he mean that he didn't intend them to meet again? she wondered—perhaps it would be as well if she believed that. She went on, her voice stiff with her efforts to keep it casual: 'Thank you for being so helpful—I don't know what I should have done without you. It was strange that we should have met again, wasn't it?'

'Not strange at all,' he corrected her. 'These things are meant. Do you know your Tennyson? Doesn't he say something about: "Ask me no more: thy fate and mine are sealed..."' He stared at her for a long moment. 'You're twenty-five, Araminta, and I am almost forty. Fifteen years is a big difference—not for me, perhaps, but for you, with those great blue eyes and golden hair.' He sighed, and she sought for words to tell him that the years didn't matter at all, that she was quite sure, but before she could speak Crispin had got to his feet. 'Don't say anything,' he begged her. 'When you're back in England, whatever you feel now, you will probably forget me.'

A remark so unjust that she almost cried out in protest. But he gave her no chance to speak, but caught her by the arm and marched her to the door for all the world as though he wanted to be rid of her. All of a sudden he had become remote and ill-humoured—she knew that whatever she said, she wouldn't be able to reach him. She allowed herself to be driven back to the flat, chattering in a meaningless fashion as they went, desperate that he shouldn't see that she was hurt and bewildered as well as angry. She had been given no chance…

He took the key from her at the flat door and opened it for her. 'Jos will be here at half past ten,' he told her. He was the casual, kind-hearted friend again; his kiss was light and quick and meant nothing at all. He was whistling as he went back down the stairs.

Araminta went to bed and cried herself to sleep. How could a girl tell a man she loved him when he didn't want to be told? She woke up in the morning with a fearful headache, and the knotty problem, returning the moment she opened her eyes, made it even worse.

It was raining when she opened the door of her little flat, and she put on all the lights and turned on the gas fire before she took off her coat. The place looked more cheerful then. A cup of tea, she told herself resolutely, fighting an overpowering loneliness, and then she would telephone her father and let him know that she was home again. She went through to the bedroom with her case; she would unpack presently, it was still early afternoon and there was nothing for her to do for the rest of the day. She shied away from the thought. It was a good thing that she was going on duty in the morning; there was nothing like hard work to make the days go quickly. She sat down to drink her tea and think about her journey. It had been easy; Jos had arrived at the flat in good time to drive her to Schiphol. Thomas had gone to work by then, bidding her a grudging goodbye and an even more grudging thanks, so that Jos's appearance had cheered her up a little. He wasn't a chatty man, but he answered her small talk with respectful monosyllables, saw to her luggage and her ticket, and bought her a pile of magazines before seeing her off in a fatherly manner, waiting until she was aboard the plane. She had turned to look for him at the last moment and had seen him in the distance and waved goodbye. Not just to him, but to a great many other things as well. She refused to put them into coherent thought.

She got up at last, washed the tea things and went to unpack. She would have to go to the shops, for there was nothing in the house to eat and she would never have time to shop in the morning; she would have to go and see Miss Best too. She sighed. The prospect of returning to St Katherine's had suddenly become dull and uninteresting. Perhaps a change of job? Another part of the country, or a week or so at Dunster? She toyed with the idea and rejected it just as the door bell rang.

It might be Sylvia, or one or her many friends, off duty and come to see how she was getting on. But it wasn't anyone she knew but a messenger boy, thrusting a long rush basket at her.

'For me?' Araminta asked, surprised.

'Miss Shaw, ain't yer?' And when she nodded: 'Sign 'ere, miss.'

She signed, found her purse and gave him something for his trouble and carried the basket into the sitting room. It was packed with roses, red and pink, cream and white; two dozen at least, and here was a card with them, inscribed disappointingly: 'Araminta, instead of goodbye. C.v.S.'

She arranged them in all the vases she possessed while she ruminated on the words. They could mean several things, and taking all in all, the most likely seemed to her that Crispin had sent the roses as a nice way of letting her know that he had thought better of it;

that although he had liked her—more than liked, perhaps—it hadn't been enough... She wept a little into the sweet-smelling flowers, then blew her nose vigorously, arranged the vases round the room, and went out shopping. But it was no use. Crispin filled her head to the exclusion of all else. She had been a fool not to have shouted him down when he had bidden her to say nothing. The arrogance of the man, she fumed, telling her what to do and what not to do and then sending her roses, so that her state of uncertainty was worse now than it had ever been. She banged and thumped her possessions in her little home in a very fury of exasperation, cooked herself a deplorable meal, which she didn't eat, and went early to bed.

She was instantly plunged into work the next morning. The Accident Room filled up as fast as it was emptied, and it was with difficulty that Araminta managed to get away to see Miss Best; a purely formal interview, with that lady expressing her sympathy at Thelma's death and at the same time declaring her satisfaction at Araminta being back at her post once more. She added a rider to the effect that the department had been very busy during her absence, and Araminta, remembering the queue waiting for attention in the Accident Room, made a suitable rejoinder and got herself back on duty, to be kept fully occupied for the rest of that day.

Two days slid by, nasty, dark November days, not quite winter yet, but bleak enough. Araminta, caught up in a vast amount of paper work, was thankful to have every minute of her time filled, so that by the time she went off duty each evening she was too tired to do more than cook herself a meal, do a few household chores and go to bed, but on her fourth morning back James stopped her as she was going to lunch, hurrying down the long passage which could lead her eventually to the nurses dining room. She would have passed him with a word of greeting, for they saw each other often enough during their working hours, but he stopped her.

'I never have the chance to talk to you,' he complained, 'and I know this is short notice, but will you come along to the Butterfly'—a favourite café frequented by the hospital staff—'this evening?' He looked suddenly rather shy. 'I've got engaged—you don't know her, but I'd like you to meet. There'll be quite a few there—you know them all. It's by way of being a celebration.'

She beamed at him. 'James, you dark horse, and how splendid! Of course I'll come. What time?' 'Seven o'clock. Come back here to the main entrance—several of us will be going at the same time, there'll be plenty of room for you in one of the cars. Mary has to come from Woolwich, so her father is going to run her up here.'

'It sounds fun. I'll be there on the dot of seven o'clock.'

She very nearly wasn't, though; an R.T.A. came in at five o'clock and it took all of the next hour to get the three people involved examined, X-rayed, tidied up and sent to their appropriate wards. Araminta cleared away with Dolly's help, made sure that the two student nurses were getting everything ready for anything else which might come in, handed over the keys to her faithful staff nurse and tore back to her flat, where, after a hasty cup of tea, she set about getting herself ready for the evening's outing. The other girls had decided to wear long dresses, so she put on the russet velvet pinafore with a chiffon blouse beneath it, piled her hair, did her face in record time, flung on the black velvet coat she had had for years, and walked briskly back to the hospital. It wanted five minutes to the hour as she went through the main doors, but James was there, looking nervous in his best suit.

His face cleared when he saw her. 'The others went on. I thought you might be a bit late—you must have moved like lightning.'

Araminta was still some way from him, so that she raised her voice to answer. 'I did—I was in a panic that I'd never make it in time. I've been looking forward to our evening all day.' She started towards him and then paused to look back over her shoulder because the doors had swung open behind her.

Crispin had come in. She forgot James and his party, she forgot where she was; her pretty face glowed with her delight at the sight of him. She choked on all the things she wanted to say; all she managed was: 'Oh, it's you!'

'Indeed, it is I.' His voice was bland and icy and she saw that his face was dark with rage, so that she faltered in her headlong rush towards him. He continued nastily: 'I'm delighted to see that you are enjoying yourself, Araminta. Don't let me keep you.' His dark eyes flickered towards James and he nodded carelessly.

'Oh, but it doesn't matter,' declared Araminta, lightheaded with her joy still and choosing her words badly. 'James won't mind…'

'How accommodating of him.' The doctor's handsome mouth was touched by an unpleasant smile. 'I had no idea that you were so fickle, Araminta.'

The smile became so ferocious that she blinked, quite bereft of words. By the time she had thought of something to say to this, he had gone. She watched his broad back disappear down the corridor leading to the consultants' room and the look on her face prompted the kindly James to ask: 'Shall I go after him, Araminta? I think he misunderstood…'

'Of course he misunderstood,' she said fierily, 'and I wouldn't go after him for all the money in the Bank of England.' She tossed her head so defiantly that her topknot looked to be in danger of coming down. 'Let's go,' she said in a bright voice which nicely disguised her wish to burst into tears.

James gave her an anxious look. 'I say, would you rather not come? I mean, he'll be back presently—he's bound to come this way.'

The very words needed to stoke up Araminta's temper. 'And find me waiting?' she demanded in a high voice. Her lovely eyes flashed. 'You're mistaken, James, I wasn't expecting Doctor van Sibbelt, you know—I had no idea that he was in England. We—we met in Amsterdam.' With a considerably heightened colour she cried: 'Oh, do let's go. Your Mary will think you've cried off, and that would never do.' She laughed so gaily at this witticism that James, who was a nice young man, laughed with her out of politeness.

Araminta got through the evening very credibly. She laughed and talked and toasted James and Mary, contributing her share of the gaiety of the occasion, and only when it was over and one of the house doctors had taken her back to her flat and she was alone again did she allow herself to think. It was already after midnight, but she sat straight down, still in her velvet coat and without even bothering to put on the gas fire, for at the back of her head was the foolish thought that Crispin might come. She waited patiently, occupying the time in trying out suitable explanations to offer him, wondering at the same time if she should have swallowed her pride and waited for him there in the hall until his return, but when she heard the clock strike one she knew that he wouldn't come and she went to bed, to lie awake for a long time, trying to make up her mind if she should write to him. Perhaps he was still in London. She would ask old Charlie, the head porter, in the morning. He might even seek her out…she slept on the happy thought.

She had no chance to see Charlie until the morning was well advanced. Staff Getty had a day off, leaving them short-handed. Charlie heard her out and then shook his bald head. 'He's gorn, Sister—spent the night and went 'arf n'hour ago. I seen 'im leave.' He eyed her with some curiosity. "oo wants 'im?'

'No one, Charlie,' Araminta said hastily. 'It's just that Doctor Hickory saw him yesterday evening and wondered why he was here.' She turned away and then paused. 'Any messages for me, Charlie?' she asked casually.

He looked across at the row of pigeonholes behind him. 'No, Sister.'

Araminta hurried back to the Accident Room to find a merciful lull in the work, so that she was able to go to her office and get the daily book up to date, make up the list of instruments for repair, engage in a slight altercation with the CSU, and embark on the off duty lists for the next two weeks. She didn't get far with this, however, for her thoughts turned to Crispin. She wasn't a conceited girl, she didn't think it likely that he had come to London for the express purpose of seeing her, but at least he could have made some effort to see her—even a note or a telephone call. Surely if a man sent roses to a girl, he would, given the chance, at least pass the time of day with her? He had been in a filthy temper, too.

She squashed a rising desire to telephone him then and there and find out exactly what was the matter. A hare-brained idea, for she hadn't a clue where he might be. Not that he would tell her; she could imagine his mouth, set like a rat trap in his dark face. She paused to draw a not very good likeness of him on her blotting pad; on second thoughts, there was nothing really wrong with a rat trap, and most of the time his mouth was rather nice, with a quirk at the corners as though he were on the point of smiling. Her reflections were interrupted here by one of the student nurses with the news that there was another overdose coming in. Araminta closed her books and started to roll up her sleeves. 'They always come just when we're due to go to dinner,' she said testily, and sailed away to check that everything was in readiness.

Thinking about it afterwards, she had no idea when the preposterous idea first entered her head; she only knew that it was there, taking shape during the afternoon, so that by the time she went to tea she knew exactly what she was going to do.

She did it the following morning as soon as Miss Best was available, and that lady heard her out with outward calm at least.

'You have some other job in mind, Sister Shaw?' she asked finally.

'No,' said Araminta, 'it's just that I want to leave London for a time—perhaps for always—I don't know yet.'

Miss Best looked mystified, but said gamely: 'Very well, if your mind is quite made up, Sister. You have three weeks' holiday due to you, have you not? Would you prefer to work the full month and receive a salary for those weeks, or leave—let me see—in five days' time?'

'Five days' time,' said Araminta quickly before Miss Best could think better of her offer.

Her superior blinked. 'Sister Dawes is capable of taking over your work permanently?' And when Araminta said yes: 'And do you consider Staff Nurse Getty suitable for the post of Junior Sister in her place?'

'Oh, rather,' Araminta agreed. 'She's jolly good at her job.'

At least Sylvia and Dolly would be happy, especially Dolly, who had been such a faithful right hand and longed, without making a thing of it, to get her Sister's blue. Dismissed by Miss Best, she went back to the department and when the opportunity occurred, invited her two colleagues into the office and over their morning coffee broke the news. It surprised her that they really minded her going, even though it would mean their own promotion, and James, when he was told, was flatteringly put out. Araminta had always been popular, now she was a little shattered to find how many of her friends were sorry to see her go. Of course they wanted to know why she should suddenly want to leave for no reason at all, and she had no answer for them, indeed she wasn't sure of the answer herself. Only she had an instant need to get away from St Katherine's and London, because if she stayed, sooner or later she might meet Crispin, and if he was going to smile at her like that again and call her fickle she wouldn't be able to bear it. She couldn't bear it now, just thinking about it.

She lived through the five days in a state of nerves in case he should appear suddenly once more, but he didn't. She said goodbye to her friends, handed over the key to her flat to Sylvia, who had begged to take it over, promised Miss Best that if she should reconsider her decision to give up nursing, she would let her know, got into the Mini and drove herself down to Somerset.

CHAPTER SEVEN

ARAMINTA HAD WARNED her father and Aunt Martha of her plans, but she strongly suspected that they hadn't believed her to be serious about them. A week or so at home, Aunt Martha had said over the telephone, would do her a great deal of good—dear Thelma's death had upset her; they would have a nice little talk about everything when she got home. Araminta, driving out of London, frowned uneasily. She had told her elderly relations very little about Thomas and now she wondered just how much she had better say about him.

She stopped for lunch on the way, for she had planned to arrive just before tea; talking over a meal was always easier and her father and aunt would both be rested after their afternoon nap. The road was surprisingly empty and she didn't hurry, but when she reached Dunster she felt her delight at seeing it again, its street almost empty, although the shops were cheerfully lighted. There were lights shining from her home too and the front door was opened as she stopped the car. She could see her aunt in the doorway; she got out of the Mini and ran to meet her.

They were glad to have her, too, they made that plain, but they were also mystified as to why she should give up a perfectly good job apparently on impulse. Over their leisurely tea she told them a good deal about her stay in Amsterdam, taking care not to dwell too much on Thomas. Just the same, when she had finished, her father observed: 'I never liked him—I told you that, did I not? But I'm glad you went, my dear, you must have been a joy to Thelma. You say you went with her to the hospital. Could the doctors there do nothing to help—with Thomas, I mean?'

'Oh, yes—they did all they could; talked to him and advised him, but you see, he wouldn't take any notice of them.'

'Were they nice? The doctors, I mean?' asked Aunt Martha.

'Very nice—and so kind. Thelma liked them all.'

'I suppose you didn't see that nice man who rescued you at Mousehole?'

Araminta took some cake she didn't want because it gave her time to think up a casual answer. 'As a matter of fact,' she told her listeners, 'he was the consultant in charge of Thelma's case.'

'Now there's a coincidence,' declared her aunt happily. 'Talk about the world being small! I expect he was very glad to see you again.'

'He didn't say,' said Araminta truthfully. 'He was very kind to Thelma.' There was a short silence while they both looked at her. Presently Aunt Martha said briskly: 'A holiday will do you good, child. You look tired—and you couldn't have come at a better time, with Christmas only six weeks away and the puddings and mincemeat to make, I shall be glad of your help.'

Araminta expressed an entirely false pleasure at her aunt's suggestion. Six weeks to Christmas and she had no job—her own silly fault—and no future without Crispin. Oh, she would make all the puddings and pies Aunt Martha could wish for and cut out the interesting bits in *The Times* for her father so that he could paste them in his reference books, and in a little while, because they really did expect it of her, she would go away and find herself another job exactly like the last one, and in a year or two her hair would lose its brightness and instead of being slim she would be bony, and bad-tempered with it.

'You look melancholy, my dear,' her aunt said sharply, so that she hastily rearranged her features into a light-hearted smile, while strongly denying any feeling other than that of pleasure at being home again.

And it was a pleasure. The calm routine of the small household was very soothing. She found herself, after the first two days, absorbed into it without any effort at all, helping with the small chores, doing the shopping, painstakingly cutting up the fruit for Aunt Martha's puddings. It was on the third morning after her arrival, with her father and aunt in Minehead, visiting the tailor and the dentist, and Araminta busy in the kitchen, that she went to answer the thud of the old-fashioned door-knocker. The baker, she supposed, not bothering to take off the old-fashioned pinny she was wearing.

It was Crispin, large and elegant, with the faintest of smiles twitching the corners of his mouth; not at all the kind of smile he had given her in the entrance hall of St Katherine's—She frowned at the awful memory of it, even while her very bones melted at the sight of him.

'Good morning,' she said coldly, steeling her loving heart.

The doctor eased himself nearer the door. 'I've come

to apologise,' he said, quite humbly for him, 'if necessary on bended knee—er—perhaps a length of sackcloth and a few ashes if you have them handy?' He peered over her shoulder into the narrow hall beyond. 'If I might come in?'

Araminta had perforce to give way before his bulk, standing on one side as he passed her, saying peevishly to him: 'Oh, all right, but you'll have to come into the kitchen—I'm cooking.'

'Ah, yes—the apron. Lunch, dear girl? I didn't stop on the way down.'

She turned round sharply, which was a mistake, for he was right behind her and she found her nose in his waistcoat. 'Your car,' she said with dignity. 'You can't leave it in the street, it's too narrow.'

'I didn't—the grocer on the corner very kindly allowed me to park beside his shop.'

They had reached the kitchen and she went to the stove to peer in her saucepans and open the oven door. The doctor's splendid nose flared. 'Roast beef?' he enquired hopefully.

'Baked potatoes, Yorkshire pudding, sprouts,' Aramita recited, shutting the oven door on the delicious aroma and going to the table. She didn't look at him, but picked up a rolling pin and attacked the pastry before her.

'Apple pie for afters?' went on the doctor, still hopeful, 'with thick cream?' He sighed in a dramatic way. 'I'm hungry.' He leaned over and picked up a pastry crumb and ate it. 'Of course it wouldn't do for you to invite me to lunch, would it? Not until we're on speaking terms again, and if I apologise now, you, being you, my dear, will probably think that I have done so merely in order to get a good wholesome meal.'

Araminta giggled; she hadn't meant to, it sent her dignity crumbling as she peeped at him sideways. 'Oh, Crispin,' she uttered, torn between exasperation and amusement, 'you're incorrigible!' She might have said a good deal more, only he had taken the rolling pin from her hand and put his arms around her, floury hands and all.

'I was abominable to you,' he said quietly, not smiling now. 'I had no right to speak to you like that, and none of it was true. But there you were, apparently on the point of spending a cosy evening with another man—a young man, too, and I'd come hell for leather to see you.'

She glowed at the words, although she answered him soberly enough. 'I was going to James' engagement party, he was giving me a lift.' She went on slowly: 'I spent a miserable evening—I hope you did, too.'

'Vixen—of course I did.' He swooped and kissed her lingeringly. 'You looked so young, my dearest girl, and I felt so very middle-aged. Just for a little while I made up my mind that I would never see you again, and then I found that I couldn't do it—you are so exactly what I want—have always wanted.' He tilted her chin and looked into her eyes. 'But am I right for you, I wonder? Set in my ways and used to doing exactly what I like with my life, and ill-tempered to boot.'

'I don't care…' began Araminta, but he stopped her.

'No, don't say it, not yet, my dear. Do you know why I came?'

'To see me?' she asked anxiously.

'That, yes, but also to ask you to come back with me and stay in my house, so that you may get to know me.'

'But I know you already,' she protested strongly. 'Crispin, I'm not a child…'

His smile was tender. 'No, perhaps not, only a green girl. Will you do as I ask? No ties, no strings, I promise you. Tante Maybella will love to have your company and we will be together as often as I can arrange it. And when you are sure that you can be happy with me, I shall ask you to marry me, and if you aren't sure, then you shall come home again and everything will be as it was before we met.' He let her go and the smile changed to a grin. 'May I stay to lunch?' he asked.

She said: 'Yes, of course,' in what she hoped was a normal voice, while she swallowed disappointment. A cleverer girl than she would have known how to make him marry her out of hand. She had done her best to tell him that she loved him, but he hadn't let her say it. Perhaps he didn't want her to, and he hadn't said that he loved her. She said steadily: 'I'd like to come very much. I expect you know that I've given up my job at St Katherine's—I was going to have a few weeks here and then look for something else.'

She finished rolling the pastry and laid it neatly over the apples lying in the dish, and the doctor went to sit on the edge of the table beside her. 'Well, you can spend a few weeks with us instead,' he assured her comfortably. His voice was very placid; he could have been an old family friend, having a chat about the weather.

It was all arranged very easily. To Araminta's surprise neither her father nor her aunt raised even the faintest of objections, but then it would have been difficult for them to have done so, for Crispin, when she had introduced him, had said calmly: 'It is delightful to meet you again. You must wonder why I am here, Mr Shaw. I have asked Araminta to come back to Amsterdam with me and stay with us—my aunt and myself. I want to marry her, but she has had very little opportunity of knowing me. I should like her to have that opportunity before I ask her.'

He had taken her hand in his while he had been speaking and held it fast, and she had stifled the thought that he still hadn't told her that he loved her. Perhaps he took it for granted that if he said that he wanted to marry her, it would mean that he loved her too.

Later on, when they were alone together, she had wanted to ask him that, but in the face of his placid friendliness, she had found it impossible.

They went, all four of them, to the Luttrell Arms for dinner that evening, and it was obvious before the evening was out that Aunt Martha was as wax in Crispin's hands, and that Mr Shaw, while saying little, took it for granted that they would marry. Indeed, when they were back home again and Crispin had left them to return to the hotel, he made the observation that Crispin was a man of intellect and good sense and one whom he would gladly welcome as a son-in-law. It was a pity, he added, that more young couples didn't get to know each other in such a sensible fashion before marrying—a view to which Araminta couldn't subscribe. Surely, her heart argued, if you loved someone, that was all that mattered? Crispin had called her a green girl, but she was twenty-five, a grown woman, and if he imagined that she was just infatuated, he was quite mistaken. She thought about it, upstairs in her bedroom, getting ready for bed; she had never been more sure of anything in her life before—it was a pity that Crispin couldn't be made to see that. Perhaps things would be easier once she was staying in the house in Amsterdam—there might be opportunities. She lay in bed, sleepily thinking up a few.

Crispin came after breakfast, wished her good morning and accepted her father's invitation to glance at some interesting documents concerning the history of the village. Araminta watched the two men disappear with mixed feelings. True, Crispin had kissed her, but it had been a very ordinary, quick kiss which meant nothing; perhaps he was a man who didn't like to be demonstrative. It struck her that he had been quite right, she really knew very little about him.

She made the beds, dusted the sitting room and went to make the coffee, while her aunt arranged the best cups and saucers and rubbed up the silver spoons—proof, if further proof were needed, that she entirely approved of Crispin.

Mr Shaw continued to discourse on local history while they drank their coffee, to the exclusion of all else, so that his daughter viewed him with a jaundiced eye and wished that he would stop, and her humour was hardly improved by the sight of Crispin, apparently enjoying every word of it. It was Aunt Martha who broke in firmly, reminding her brother that if Araminta didn't go to the shops there would be no lunch that day, and since Crispin was interested in the village, what better opportunity of his seeing it for himself while accompanying Araminta.

This sensible remark had the desired effect. Araminta whipped up to her room to put on her coat, and when she got down again, Crispin had his coat on too and was in the hall, holding the shopping basket.

She felt a little shy at first, going in and out of the butcher's and the baker's; choosing cauliflowers and apples and grapes at the greengrocers, but her companion appeared perfectly at home in his new role and when they had delivered the basket to Aunt Martha, suggested that a walk might be pleasant. It was a splendid morning, cold and windy, but the sun was shining as they bent their steps towards the church, where they wandered round while Araminta called to mind all she knew of the Luttrell family and the monks who had lived in Dunster so long ago. 'They were in the hotel, you know,' she told him. 'It's really very old. The village is lovely, isn't it, and so is the church.'

He took her hand and slowed her walk to a halt. 'Would you wish to marry here, Araminta?'

She had had her dreams like any other girl. 'Well, yes, though I don't think it matters where you marry, as long as you love each other.'

He only smiled faintly. 'I expect you're right. Where do we go next?'

He wasn't going to let her say that she loved him; she wondered fleetingly if he was afraid that she might regret it. With an effort she kept her voice friendly and nothing more. 'We can go through the castle grounds, if you like—they're not open to the public, but no one minds if the village people take the short cut through the wood to the main road.'

It was pretty amongst the trees. Far in front of them they could hear the traffic on the main road between Minehead and Bridgewater, but here it was quiet except for the wind whistling and moaning between the leafless branches. The path was narrow, and Araminta, who knew it like the palm of her hand, went in front, pausing every now and again to explain some part of the terrain when it came into view, but when they reached the edge of the wood and paused to look beyond the road to the grey, wind-tossed water of the Bristol

Channel, Crispin put an arm across her shoulders and drew her close.

'Will you be ready to come back with me tomorrow?' he asked.

'Tomorrow?' She turned to look up into his face. 'But Father might…'

'He assured me that he could see no possible objection; it is for you to say, my dear.'

She smiled at him. 'It was just that I'm surprised—everything's happening so quickly. What time do you want to leave?'

'In the early afternoon—we'll go from Harwich.' He turned her round to face him. 'Your second visit to Amsterdam will be quite different from your first,' he promised, and kissed her with a gentleness which sent the tears to her eyes, so that she had to look away quickly in case he should see. 'I'm looking forward to it,' she told him quietly, and then: 'We've time to go down to the water, we only have to cross the road at the bottom of the hill and go down that lane.'

They walked fast, arm-in-arm into the wind, talking about a great many things, and Araminta was glad to discover that they agreed about most of them. They got back to the house just in time to drink their sherry before lunch, and when it was eaten, Crispin washed up in the manner of someone who did so every day of his life, something which Araminta doubted very much, before saying that he had one or two matters to attend to and might he come back for tea? She had no idea what the matters might be and he didn't enlighten her, but he looked remarkably pleased with himself when he returned.

He took her out to dinner again that evening and she wore the dress she had most fortuitously seen in the smart little boutique in the main street. It was very pretty; of crêpe, its colour a shade darker than her hair. It fell in tiny pleats from a high-necked yoke and its wide belt made her slim waist seem even slimmer.

'Very pretty,' observed Crispin when she joined him, and she wasn't sure if he meant her person or her dress, but it was a good beginning to an evening which became better and better as its hours slipped away. They took their time over dinner, for at this time of year there were few guests at the hotel. The food was superb and the dining room warm and softly lighted, and when they had finished they crossed the narrow, flagstoned hall to the coffee lounge, happily empty, and had coffee before the blazing log fire while they talked comfortably about nothing in particular. It seemed to Araminta that she was discovering a number of aspects of Crispin's character she had never considered before. She had, until now, thought of him as a doctor first and as a man—a rather remote, ill-tempered man—second; now he was letting her catch glimpses of the man and she had liked what she had seen very much—and that, she reminded herself, had nothing to do with loving him.

They set off the next day, with one of Aunt Martha's excellent lunches inside them and Araminta's largest case in the boot. She hadn't been sure what to pack, so in the end she had taken an armful of sweaters, some slacks, her newish tweed suit, her thick coat and the jersey dress, and naturally she had added the new crêpe; anything else she would have to buy while she was in Amsterdam; she had sufficient money for that.

She settled into the comfort of the Rolls' front seat with a sigh of pleasure and only the faintest twinge of anxiety that things might not work out right, after all.

She buoyed herself up with the promise that it wouldn't be her fault if they didn't and decided wisely not to allow her mind to dwell on it too much. She waved to her family, gave Crispin a small, loving smile and gave herself over to the pleasure of a long journey in his company.

By the time they had reached Harwich and were safely on board, she felt as though she had known him all her life. She told him so before going below to her cabin and his answering smile had been charming, although he had given her a searching look. 'That's the object of the exercise,' he reminded her blandly. 'Sleep well.'

Surprisingly, she did, and even the darkness of the six o'clock morning couldn't damp her good spirits. It was only just getting light by the time they reached Amsterdam, fifty miles away, but there were already lights shining from the windows of Crispin's home, and Jos, with Rikki beside him, was there to welcome them.

'Breakfast,' said the doctor. 'Can we have it in ten minutes, Jos? I expect Miss Shaw would like to go to her room first.' He turned to look at her. 'Will that suit you, Araminta?'

She said shyly that it would, and followed Frone upstairs to the same room as she had had before. There were fresh flowers there, even English magazines and a newspaper, and everything she could possibly need in the bathroom. She looked at everything in a happy daze, tidied her hair in a perfunctory fashion and went downstairs again and found Crispin waiting for her in the hall. As they went into the pleasant little room where they had breakfasted together before, she asked: 'Do you have to go to the hospital today?'

'Not until the afternoon, but I've some patients to see

privately this morning.' She handed him his coffee and he asked: 'Forgive me if I run through my letters?'

She sat like a mouse, drinking cup after cup of delicious coffee and eating her croissant while she watched him. He looked as though he had slept the night through and had had all the leisure in the world to achieve the impeccable appearance he now presented. Araminta suspected that he had what Aunt Martha would call an iron constitution, able to do without sleep and food and still present a calm, elegant front to the world; a resourceful man too, but once roused, of a very nasty temper. She loved every inch of him.

He looked up suddenly and caught her staring. 'I'm abominably rude,' he told her, and stacked his letters neatly. 'I'll be back about six o'clock this evening. If you're not too tired, shall we go out after dinner? The shops will be shut, but they'll be lighted, and you might enjoy looking at them.'

'Oh, I'd love that—but wouldn't it bore you?'

He answered her gravely: 'When I'm with you I'm never bored, Araminta. Tante Maybella will be down at about half past ten—get her to show you the house, there's nothing she enjoys more, and you might find it interesting.'

Araminta beamed at him. 'Crispin, you're such a nice man!' She added worriedly: 'I do hope I fit in…'

He got out of his chair and came round the table and bent to kiss her cheek as he said laughingly: 'You fit in quite perfectly.' He dropped a second kiss on top of her head, said *'Tot ziens,'* and was gone.

She unpacked first and then had a bath, made fragrant by Madame Rochas, put on a skirt and sweater, did her hair and face very carefully, then went downstairs. She was crossing the hall slowly, wondering where she should go, when Jos appeared.

'There is a fire in the small sitting room,' he informed her, and ushered her into a room—not small at all, according to her standards, with a large bow window overlooking the garden at the back of the house. It was furnished very comfortably with a number of armchairs and sofas, a richly piled carpet upon the floor, and a profusion of paintings upon its walls. Araminta rather liked it, and so apparently did Rikki, who in company with the tabby cat was stretched out before the fire.

'Shall I take the dog, miss?' asked Jos.

'Oh, no—please don't, she's such good company.' She smiled and received an answering smile from the craggy face.

'Then I'll bring you some coffee, miss; Mevrouw van Sibbelt will be down any minute now.'

The old lady arrived with the coffee tray. She was still wearing black, but this morning her dress was of a fine wool, with a little white pleated frill round the high collar. She was wearing her gold chains, though, and a small enamelled watch fastened by a brooch to the tucked bodice. She looked like a small porcelain doll with her beautifully dressed hair and pink and white complexion.

Araminta was a little surprised at the warmth of her welcome, for she still had some fleeting doubts as to her hostess's true feelings towards her, but now she began to think that she must have imagined them, for the morning was passed delightfully, chatting over coffee, and then by an inspection of the house. Mevrouw van Sibbelt, surprisingly nimble for her eighty-odd years, led the way in and out of rooms which Araminta found surprisingly beautiful; they were seldom used, explained her guide, only when Crispin gave a party, or invited his numerous cousins, aunts and uncles to visit him on the Feast of Sint Nicolaas, or to stay over Christmas and the New Year. 'New Year is the most enjoyable,' declared Mevrouw van Sibbelt, 'for the house looks so splendid and every room is in use, there are so many people…'

'You act as hostess?' asked Araminta gently.

'Indeed I do—a task I thoroughly enjoy.' The old lady paused to enjoy a reverie of her own and then said brightly: 'You will like the ballroom, it is along there—if you would open those double doors, Araminta…'

It was a splendid apartment, very formal, with its gilded pillars and silk-panelled walls. It was at the back of the house, reached by a short passage over-looking one side of the garden. Araminta twirled on its polished floor, imagining herself in a really super dress, dancing with Crispin—apricot chiffon would do very nicely, with some really beautiful embroidery. She gave a final twirl and came to a laughing halt in front of her companion, and was shocked by the expression she surprised on the old face—not hate, exactly, not even dislike, but a look of speculation tinged with fear, and what could Mevrouw van Sibbelt, living in the lap of luxury in her nephew's house, have to be afraid of? Araminta stopped in mid-twirl and asked anxiously: 'Is anything the matter, Mevrouw?'

The look had gone even as she spoke; it was just an elderly face once more, gently smiling at her. 'Of course not, my dear, just a twinge in my bones, I expect—natural enough at my age, is it not? It's a little frightening to grow old. One becomes useless…'

Araminta took a small, beringed hand in hers. 'You

are certainly not useless, Mevrouw van Sibbelt, and you have no need to be frightened. You have Crispin and he loves you very much.' She would have liked to have added 'And you will have me too,' but it seemed presumptuous to say that.

Mevrouw van Sibbelt smiled then. 'You're a nice child,' she declared, 'and not at all like any of the others.'

Araminta didn't ask who the others were. Her companion was obviously speaking about the other girls whom Crispin must have brought to his home from time to time. And why not? she asked herself stoutly. He had been free to do as he liked and have the friends he chose, had he not? It was a pity that this charitable sentiment should have been entirely swamped by a great wave of jealousy; she hated herself for it.

'It takes all kinds to make a world,' she pronounced in a bright voice. 'Where do we go next, or would you like to rest for a little while?'

'The first floor, I think.' Mevrouw van Sibbelt was looking at her with faint disappointment. 'For a young girl you have very little curiosity,' she said tartly, and when Araminta didn't answer, went on: 'After lunch I shall take my little rest, perhaps you would like to explore the rest of the house then. Let us go back the way we came and go up the main staircase.'

By the time they had reached the head of the stairs, her little flash of ill humour had vanished and they spent the next hour wandering through the rooms which led off the gallery which ran round three sides of the hall. They didn't go into all of them; Mevrow van Sibbelt paused before the arched door with its swags of fruit and flowers carved above it and which dominated one side of the gallery and explained that it was the principal bedroom of the house and not in use. 'It will be a different matter when Crispin marries,' she said, and peered sideways at Araminta. 'It is a very a lovely room.'

She led the way to another door and opened that instead. 'This is one of the guest rooms—charming, is it not?'

Araminta looked around her. The room was certainly that, with its heavy Beidermeier furniture and the pale pastel silk of the curtains and bedspread. She began to wonder, a little uneasily, just how rich a man Crispin was; much richer than she had imagined, she realised that now as they continued their inspection of one room after the other, each perfection and all apparently ready for instant occupation. Presently they went down to lunch together in the small room in which she had breakfasted, and over their omelettes and fruit, discussed the house and its treasures, and the old lady, quite forgetting her nap, lingered long after they were finished, talking of her youth and the balls she had attended and telling of the family's history. Araminta sat enthralled; anything to do with Crispin interested her, and this was his home and his family… She watched her companion mount the staircase for her long delayed rest with a feeling of real regret.

But there was the second floor, and when she reached it presently it was to find that it was almost exactly similar to the one below, save that here, at the back of the house, there was a nursery wing. A large, high-ceilinged room, overlooking the garden and beyond that, a canal and an interesting vista of gabled rooftops. A smaller room led from it, as did a bathroom, tiny kitchen and two much smaller rooms. 'Enough for six children,' commented Araminta, aloud, 'with a couple of nursemaids thrown in.'

There was a cupboard along one wall and after a moment's hesitation she opened it, to spend an enraptured half hour looking at the toys stacked neatly away on its shelves. Some of them were very old; dolls with china heads and flaxen hair and most beautifully dressed, clockwork toys, a magnificent dolls' house, small wooden horses on wheels, a whole Noah's Ark—she inspected them all, wondering which of them had belonged to Crispin when he was a little boy and imagining the delight of future inhabitants of the nursery when they opened the cupboard doors. She heaved an unconscious sigh and went down to the drawing room and had a solitary tea, for Mevrouw van Sibbelt hadn't reappeared, before getting her coat and going into the garden to play ball with Rikki until it was dark.

Crispin was home when she went to the drawing room an hour later after changing into the jersey dress, and over their drinks engaged her in a pleasant desultory conversation, wanting to know how she had spent her day, which naturally enough led to talk of the house and its history, talk which became general when his aunt joined them, and which stayed so throughout dinner. It was after they had had their coffee and Crispin had suggested that she should get her coat that Araminta feared that the old lady was going to complain at being left alone, but he reminded her kindly that an old friend of hers would be arriving shortly. 'You won't miss us at all,' he told her, laughing. 'Besides, we shan't be late back—I've a busy day tomorrow.'

Their outing was an unqualified success. True, it had begun to drizzle with a cold rain and the wind was blowing, as Araminta had discovered it did in Holland, round every corner, but she hardly noticed it as they walked briskly through the wet streets, stopping here and there to admire the dark outline of some small bridge or a particularly impressive gable, until they reached the Kalverstraat, where Crispin obligingly shortened his stride so that she might peer into the shop windows. There were quite a lot of people strolling around, despite the weather, doing exactly as they were doing, and when she remarked on it, he said half laughing: 'I expect they're couples setting up house together, deciding what they want to buy for their homes.'

'You're got everything already,' she pointed out.

'I haven't got you, Araminta-not yet.'

It was on the tip of her tongue to tell him then and there that he had got her—had had her for quite some time, but if she did he might think her too eager. He had said that she was to stay at his home and get to know him and she had been there barely twenty-four hours; he would remind her of that if she said anything, so she kept a prudent silence, albeit with difficulty. Here was a man, she knew that now, who refused to be hurried—or rather, refused to hurry her. She swallowed everything she so longed to tell him and said gaily: 'This is fun! Most men hate looking at shops—Father would rather run a mile.'

'Well, I don't make a habit of it, Araminta, but I must admit that I'm enjoying it very much with you. Shall we have a cup of coffee somewhere?'

They were home again before Tante Maybella's visitor had gone. Araminta was introduced to the lady, a large, rather plain-faced woman with an overwhelming bosom and an air of consequence. She smiled kindly at Araminta, engaged her in conversation in excellent English, addressed a few laughing remarks to Crispin and took her leave, and very shortly afterwards, Mevrouw van Sibbelt went to her bed.

'I think I'll go to bed too,' said Araminta. 'I daresay you've got some work or something or other to read.'

The doctor looked up from tickling Rikki's ear. 'Indeed I have—why not come and keep me company while I do it? There's a stove in the study and you can curl up in a chair and read too, if you have a mind to do so.'

'I won't be in your way?'

He shook his head. 'No.' He straightened up and crossed the room to stand before her. 'Do you know, I am just beginning to realise how lonely I've been?' He took her hand in his. 'It's the room next to the small sitting room—did you see it this morning?'

She shook her head. 'Your aunt said that she never went in there.'

He laughed. 'You don't find her tiresome, I hope? She is very difficult sometimes, but then she is an old lady now—I remember her when I was a little boy and she was my favourite aunt.' He added thoughtfully: 'She was always so kind…'

Araminta looked up into his dark face. 'You're a kind man yourself,' she told him gravely.

The study was warm, smelled of leather and tobacco and was furnished with a giant-sized desk and chair and several comfortable armchairs drawn up to the stove. The desk, she noted, was piled high with a conglomeration of papers, notes, letters and a book or two, and once Crispin had settled her in a chair with a copy of *The Lancet* to amuse her, he sat down contentedly to work. She didn't read but watched his dark head, the silver in it showing up strongly in the lamp's light, while he wrote, occasionally telephoned, and then read his letters. She was quite startled when he said: 'It's like having a friendly mouse in the room. Rikki always comes with me, of course, but he isn't the same as a pretty girl.'

'You called me a mouse!'

He chuckled. 'A restful mouse as well as a pretty one.' He cast down the last of the letters on his desk. 'Thank you for bearing me company, Araminta.' He shot a quick look at her. 'You didn't find it too dull?'

'No, of course not, I like being here with you.'

'You enchant me,' he told her as they crossed the hall, 'but that's no reason for keeping you out of your bed.' He gave her a gentle push in the direction of the staircase. 'Good night, dear girl.'

Araminta found that the days passed quickly, although she did very little. She spent a good deal of time in Mevrouw van Sibbelt's company, ventured out by herself in the afternoons and spent her evenings with Crispin, walking Rikki in Vondelpark, driving to Schevingenen to dine and then walk along the boulevard in the cold dark, or visiting the Concertgebouw.

On the fourth afternoon after her arrival she had gone shopping, for it was obvious that her wardrobe fell far short of her requirements. She had liked the look of Krause en Vogelzang when they had been window-shopping, so now she ventured inside its elegant doors, to emerge a good while later, much lighter in the purse but deeply content with her purchase—a silk jersey dress in a soft sage green, its long sleeves gathered into deep cuffs and having a demure neckline ornamented by a chiffon bow under her chin. Just in case Crispin should find the time to take her dancing, as he had hinted the evening before, she had bought an evening dress too, of blue velvet which matched her eyes exactly, its deep neckline outlined with tiny silk frills. She counted herself fortunate in matching it exactly with velvet slippers and a velvet stole which just happened to catch her eye.

She had the opportunity to wear this charming outfit two evenings later. Crispin had telephoned during the afternoon to tell her that he had booked a table at the Amstel Hotel for dinner and dancing; he endeared himself still further to her by asking, in the nicest possible way, if she wanted a new dress for the occasion, because if so she had only to say so and he would instruct his bank.

'What a dear you are!' she exclaimed warmly, and heard his chuckle. 'As a matter of fact, I saw a dress I liked and bought it…'

She found the Amstel Hotel quietly impressive, solidly comfortable to the point of luxury and a most fitting background for the velvet dress, and it was delightful to discover that their table overlooked the Amstel River. Even on a near winter's evening, it was a pleasant sight, with the lights of countless barges and boats twinkling on its black water. Araminta turned away from watching them to find Crispin's eyes on her. 'You look delightful,' he told her. 'That's a pretty dress, and a pretty girl inside it.'

She pinkened. 'Thank you, Crispin. I—I hoped you'd like it.' She smiled shyly. 'Don't look at me like that.'

'Like what?' he asked blandly.

'Like that. Did you have a busy day?'

His eyes gleamed with amusement. 'Yes, I did. Araminta, you're shy.' His smile enfolded her, so that she smiled back at him, suddenly at her ease.

'What shall we eat?' he went on matter-of-factly. 'Shall we order now and then dance?'

They finished their drinks and danced—they danced a great deal. Araminta hardly noticed what they ate and it wasn't until her glass was being refilled that she remarked dreamily: 'It's champagne, isn't it?' which made Crispin laugh and urge her to drink up so that they could dance again. It was towards the end of the evening as they were circling the room to 'Let's dance the old-fashioned way' that he said softly: 'I couldn't agree more with this song; it's how I'd like to dance with you always, darling.' And when the music stopped, he said: 'Let's go home. I want to talk to you.'

Araminta had the pleasant sensation that she was dreaming and then waking up to find it was real. 'Yes, of course,' she agreed in a voice which trembled just a little and sped to get her wrap.

It had begun to freeze outside and she wrapped the soft velvet close as they went out to the car. They hardly spoke on the way home and she was aware of a mounting excitement as the doctor drove through the narrow streets. There were still lights showing in the house, and Jos came from the back of the hall to enquire if they would like coffee, then went away to fetch it.

Araminta allowed the doctor to take her wrap and then her hand as they went into the drawing room. It looked quite beautiful in the firelight and the soft glow of a solitary lamp; Araminta looked lovely too. Crispin eyed her with satisfaction and told her so before he kissed her soundly. 'I had no idea I was so impatient a man,' he observed. 'Will you marry me, Araminta?'

She stood within the circle of his arms, looking up at him. He was a handsome man, if one happened to like dark, beaky-nosed faces and dark, heavy-lidded eyes, and she did. They were smiling at her now in such a way that she could hardly wait to say yes, and it was a good thing that she hadn't hesitated, for she had barely uttered when the telephone rang and with an impatient word Crispin went to answer it.

Such a pity, she thought, when there was so much to say between them, and listening to his urgent, low-voiced questions. She could see that it was some knotty medical problem, that just for the moment had swept her right out of his head. It didn't surprise her in the least when he put down the receiver and said: 'There's an emergency which presents several problems. Go to bed, my dear, we'll talk tomorrow.'

He kissed her briefly, his mind already grappling with whatever awaited him at the hospital, and she, understanding very well, said quietly: 'Yes, dear? I hope it isn't anything too bad,' and stood where she was until she heard the heavy thud of the front door. Only when Jos came to take away the coffee tray did she wish him good night and make her way up to bed, still very happy; unwilling to come out of her lovely dream-like world.

When she got down in the morning, it was to find that Crispin had been home, slept for a couple of hours, breakfasted and returned to the hospital. He hoped to be back, said Jos, in the early afternoon, but there was a possibility that it might be considerably later than that. Araminta ate her breakfast, had a brisk session with Rikki in the garden and came indoors to find Mevrouw van Sibbelt in the little sitting room. The old lady seemed pleased to see her, and they spent an hour together chatting until it was suggested that Araminta might like to take a walk before their lunch. It was colder than it had been for some days, but she walked briskly, coming back with glowing cheeks and bright eyes. The glow evaporated a little when Jos met her with the news that the doctor didn't expect to get home before evening, a piece of news which took away her appetite, something which the old lady remarked upon while they were having their coffee after lunch.

'You are excited, my dear,' she smiled across the room. 'I think perhaps it is because Crispin has asked you to marry him. Am I right?'

'Well, yes, he has,' admitted Araminta, and was a little taken aback when her companion murmured: 'You are so suitable…'

'Suitable?' she echoed, rather at a loss.

The old lady smiled gently. 'You are young and strong and like children, do you not? And you find this house to your taste—Crispin would never marry a girl who would want to alter his home in any way. You are a pretty young woman too and have nice manners—and quite different from Nelissa.'

'And who is Nelissa?' asked Araminta, aware that her voice was too sharp.

'You do not know about her? She is the girl whom Crispin loved—still loves—and can never marry.'

Araminta felt an icy hand move slowly up her spine. 'Crispin will tell me about her if he wants to,' she said stoutly, and heard the hateful shake in her voice as she spoke.

The old lady peeped at her over her old-fashioned gold-rimmed spectacles. 'My dear, as you grow older you will learn that there are some things about which a man never speaks.'

'You mean I mustn't ask him?'

Her companion nodded.

'But why not? He—he wants to marry me, Mevrouw van Sibbelt.'

'Crispin is forty years old, Araminta, he knows that he must marry soon if he wishes for a son to carry on the family name, and believe me, he does wish that.' The silvery voice was decisive. 'You should count yourself fortunate he has chosen you. There are several suitable girls who would be only too glad to step into your shoes.'

'But it was me he asked,' said Araminta flatly.

'And I am glad, child—his strong feelings of pity for you in the first place, when he discovered you slaving for that cousin of yours, more than tipped the balance in your favour.' She met Araminta's outraged eye with a smile and asked in a sympathetic voice: 'Has he ever said that he loves, you, my dear?'

He never had. Araminta admitted that in a proud little voice which disdained sympathy. 'This Nelissa,' she asked in a voice as calm as she could make it, 'you said that Crispin would marry her if he could—why doesn't he?'

'There are circumstances...' said her companion mysteriously, and paused. 'A few days ago—you remember that he went away unexpectedly? I must say no more than that, only—if he had not already had an understanding with you...but he had. He made that clear when he came back from your home in England, and he is not a man to go back on his word, whatever the cost to himself.'

'So I'm standing in the way of his happiness,' said Araminta. She sat staring at the old lady, sitting there tearing her lovely dreams apart in that silvery voice. Of course the dear soul didn't realise what she was doing, and that was a good thing really, because there was still time to do something about it—only she would have to look sharp; she felt strangely numb, but her brain was clear enough and already busy with a plan. And after all, it was easy enough. Mevrouw van Sibbelt was making preparations to go upstairs for her nap and she wouldn't come down again until tea time or later, and Crispin wouldn't be back until the evening. Araminta could be miles away by then. She went upstairs with the old lady with the remark that she would get her coat and go for a walk.

In the room she snatched up her jacket and put it on, found her overnight bag, stuffed it with whatever caught her distracted eye, picked up her gloves and handbag and hurried through the quiet house and out of its door. She still felt very peculiar and her mind wasn't as clear as it should have been, which was probably why, when she reached the station and joined the ticket-buying queue, she discovered that she had left her wallet and almost all her money, as well as her passport, behind. She could go back, but the risk of encountering Jos was great and she would never be able to think up a plausible story as to why she had gone out with an overnight bag.

The woman in front of her bought a ticket to Valkenburg, and Araminta bought one too, because she remembered that it was a long way from Amsterdam, and that was important… Her state of mind didn't allow her to realise that her ticket had cost her considerably more than half the money she had with her.

CHAPTER EIGHT

ARAMINTA WAS AWARE that the time spent sitting in the train should be put to good use deciding what to do next, but her mind refused to work. She stared out of the window at the unfamiliar scenery, her head empty of anything but deep misery, and when she saw the woman who had been in front of her in the queue gather up her bags, took her own small bag from the rack, guessing that they would be nearing Valkenburg. When the train came to a halt in the well-kept station, she followed her out on to the platform, gave up her ticket and walked out into the street.

It was already dusk and the wind was decidedly fresh. She thanked heaven that she was wearing her tweed suit and a wool jumper under it, took a reassuring grip of her paltry luggage, and looked around her.

There were several hotels across the quiet street—she dismissed two of them at once; that they were spotlessly clean she had no doubt, but their black net curtains and purple lighting proclaimed them as ultra-modern and frequented by those addicted to pop music. The third hotel was large, brilliantly lighted and quite obviously much too expensive. The thought of the very small sum she had in her purse sent a shiver down her already cold spine, although it didn't weaken her resolution. Telling herself that there would be any number of small, suitably cheap hotels in a town given over almost entirely to the summer tourist trade, she started briskly for the end of the street. It led in its turn into a wider, busier thoroughfare filled with a fair amount of traffic and lined with more hotels, all regrettably closed for the winter, and so it proved with all the smaller hotels.

Araminta walked, not quite so fast now, round the main streets of the compact little town, with its ruined castle brooding over it. There were several bars open now, filled with cheerful, noisy groups, mostly men, but she was tired and the idea of wrestling with enquiries about a room which might cost too much money, and the difficulty of explaining that she could only afford a certain amount, and that before a crowd of strangers who would probably not understand a word she said, made even her stout heart quail. She retraced her steps, out of the town's centre, up the hill once more and over the level crossing by the station, feeling a little desperate. She had been a fool to leave Crispin's house without making sensible plans; without taking sufficient money with her…even as she thought that she knew that she couldn't have stayed another minute, even though it had been the silliest thing she had ever done in her whole life.

She blinked back tears, gave a defiant sniff, and looked about her. There were a few shops in the street and a number of hotels and guest-houses, all closed, but at the top of the hill there were welcoming lights. Recklessly Araminta walked towards them, longing only for a place in which to put her head for the night. They streamed invitingly from a large hotel standing back from the road; a pleasant place, surrounded by trees and flower beds. It looked warm and cheerful, and without stopping to think she made for its entrance—at least she could have a cup of coffee there.

It was delightfully warm inside and the faint clatter of knives and forks reminded her of her hunger. A little lightheaded at the thought of a meal, she went to the desk and asked if they had a room.

They had, and its cost would take all but a couple of gulden of her money, but she really didn't care any more. She filled in the form she was offered, took the key and followed the receptionist through the foyer, past the dining room and into a quiet hall, where she was advised to mount the staircase at its centre. 'Number fifty-five,' said the receptionist, and left her.

The room was small but well-furnished and warm. Araminta took out the meagre contents of her overnight bag and laid them on the bed: a nightgown, a change of undies, writing paper and envelopes—she wondered why she had put those in—a brush and comb and a bag of hastily collected toilet articles, and that was the lot. She stared at them at though by doing so she could turn them all into the things she had left behind, then picked them up despondently and arranged them on the wash-stand and in a drawer of the dressing table. Even for one uncertain night, one should remain tidy. Then she combed her hair, put her jacket back on again and went downstairs and out into the street. She had noticed a *potat frites* stall in the town—chips would be filling and only fifty cents a portion, which would leave her enough to buy a cup of coffee at the hotel before she went to bed, pay her bill and still have almost a gulden over—sufficient for a glass of milk, perhaps… She would worry about that in the morning; a good night's sleep and breakfast would give her back her usual resourcefulness and energy.

She found the stall, bought her paper poke of chips and walked along munching them. She had never eaten chips from a paper bag before and perhaps it wasn't very good manners, but they hardly mattered now; there was no one to see her, and even if there had been, she didn't care; the chips were crisp and their warmth was decidedly heartening. She polished off the last crumb and started back to the hotel, feeling much better.

She hadn't realised that there were quite so many people staying there; middle-aged and downright elderly, they sat at the small round tables covered with Persian rugs, the men drinking beer or gin, the women sipping glasses of wine. There was a band in one corner of the foyer, too; a man at the piano and another younger one, sitting in the centre of an assortment of instruments, with an accordion on his knee, and when the waitress brought her coffee she told Araminta in a mixture of Dutch and English that there was to be an evening's music for the benefit of the old people's club staying at the hotel on their annual outing.

Araminta sipped her coffee, making it last, and bent her mind to her problems, but not for long. The band, making up for its lack of size by its enthusiasm, burst into a gay tune which had everyone round her stamping and clapping and presently singing too. The noise was overpowering, but it drowned her sad, frightened thoughts while she sat on, long after her coffee cup had been drained, glad that thinking had become an impossibility.

But presently, despite her determination to stay where she was in such cheerful surroundings, her eye lids began to droop and she made her way up to her room. A good night's sleep was what she needed; she was tired and headachy and she would need a clear head in the morning. She got ready for bed, laid her head on the pillow and was instantly asleep.

She wakened in less than an hour, her mind crystal clear, ready to tackle all and every problem. Hours later, listening to a chorus of clocks chiming seven, she was forced to the conclusion that none of her problems were surmountable; ideas had raced round and round inside her weary head with all the energy of mice in a wheel, and none of them had been of any use to her at all. She got up and made a slow toilet, unable to do much to her poor white face, for she had only her powder compact and lipstick with her, then she rammed her miserable bits and pieces back into her overnight bag, and went down to breakfast.

The old people's club were making an early start for home. The more active members were already hatted and coated and waiting for the bus which would take them back to Amsterdam, while the laggards finished their breakfast. Araminta sat down for her own breakfast at a small table in a corner of the dining room and eyed the basket of assorted breads upon it with hungry pleasure. Despite her headache, she made a good breakfast, washed down by the milkless tea the waiter fetched for her, and felt all the better for it, so that when she had paid her bill and carefully counted the handful of coins which was all she had now, she still felt quite able to cope with whatever the day might bring.

During breakfast the half-formed notion that she might hitchhike her way to Rotterdam and there borrow her fare home from the British Consul had been taking shape in her mind. She had never thumbed a lift in her life, but thousands did, and if they could, so could she. She buttoned her jacket, wishing for a scarf to tie over her head, pulled on her gloves, and pot-valiant from her breakfast, left the hotel. The road north ran past the hotel. She walked along it for a mile or more until she was quite clear of the town and took up her position.

For a little while cars streamed past her, but none of them stopped. She walked on, stopping every few yards to lift her hand at a passing motorist, but her stops became less frequent, for the sky, which had been a cold, unfriendly grey since early morning, had become darker, the clouds whipped up by a mean wind. She had no idea what the time was; she had left her watch behind too—like a fool, she told herself fiercely—and she was on a stretch of road now with no houses in sight and almost no traffic. She had thought innocently enough that she had only to stand by the side of the road and lift a hand for someone to stop. That her appearance was spoiling her chances was something she hadn't guessed at; a well-dressed young woman, with neat hair and gloved hands holding a smart overnight bag, was so unlike the usual type of lifter that the majority of drivers hardly noticed her, and once or twice, when she had stepped into the road to attract attention, the irate drivers had merely shaken their fists at her.

She stood irresolutely, trying to make up her mind what to do; she could walk on and hope that sooner or later someone would stop, but supposing they didn't? She might be better off in the town, after all, and a few drops of icy rain decided her. She retraced her footsteps, making plans as she went. She would go to the police station and ask someone there to lend her enough money to get to Rotterdam... She frowned; they would want to know why she wanted the money in the first place, and when she explained, why she had left Crispin's house in such a hurry, and they would certainly want to know why she had come to Valkenburg, which was, after all, miles away from Amsterdam. If only she had gone to Rotterdam—with enough money—and gone down to the Hoek and got on a boat to Harwich, but she hadn't, and on second thoughts the police would be no good, they might even clap her in prison. She didn't know anything about Dutch Law, perhaps it was the same as France where one was sent to prison until one could prove one's innocence.

She was back in town by now and surprised to find that it was already past two o'clock. She fingered her purse. The thirty-five cents in it weren't enough for a cup of coffee, but they would be sufficient for a roll or a small bar of chocolate. Araminta settled for the roll, counting the money carefully into one hand as she crossed one of the little bridges over the narrow river which ran through the town between the shopping streets. It was sheer ill-chance that a passer-by in a hurry should bump into her so that she lost her balance, clutched at the bridge railing to keep her feet, and let every single coin in her handfall into the water below.

Araminta stared down at the sluggish little river, and being a girl of some spirit, voiced her thoughts aloud, which, while relieving her pent-up feelings, did nothing to help her. She was now quite penniless, and the sensation wasn't a pleasant one. She thought of the roll she had been going to buy with passionate longing and told herself in a loud, cross voice because there was no one to hear her: 'This is the last straw!'

But it wasn't. The very last straw of all came in the form of more icy rain; it had been falling in a desultory fashion on and off for the last hour, and now it became a sudden torrential downpour, soaking her within seconds.

There was no shelter on the bridge, but at its end she could see what appeared to be an old castle set in a small enclosure of trees and shrubs which would afford some shelter at least, she lost no time in making for it.

It was indeed a castle, half hidden by ivy and bushes against its walls, and although it was small, its vast front door stood open with steps leading down to a second door, firmly shut. But it gave some shelter. Araminta perched gingerly on the bottom step, and presently, with her bag beside her to lean her head on, she went to sleep.

It was still light when she woke up, although the doorway was considerably darkened by Crispin, whose bulk was blocking it. She couldn't see his face properly, but his voice, icy with rage, set her shivering.

'You silly little fool,' he said with suppressed violence, and she remembered in a bemused way that the very first time they had met on the patch of sand below the Cornish cliffs, he had said just that.

He leaned down and plucked her to her feet and caught up her bag. Her empty purse fell to the ground as he did so, and he picked that up too and turned it over in his gloved hand. There was no expression on his face now and she couldn't understand what he said, but it sounded violent and not quite nice, and even though she wasn't sure if she were awake or dreaming she said tartly: 'Don't you swear your beastly Dutch oaths at me!'

He gave a crack of laughter. 'Had you no money at all?' His voice still held that icy anger to make her shiver again; Araminta felt defeated and so unhappy that she had no anger left. She told him in a dreary little voice: 'I had thirty-five cents, but someone bumped into me on a bridge…it was in my hand and it fell into the water.'

She waited for him to laugh, but he only sighed deeply and said: 'The car's in the Dekkerstraat, just over the bridge. Come along.'

'No,' said Araminta—a waste of breath, for he took no notice at all, but caught her by the arm and marched her back the way she had come, back over the bridge and across the covered pavement to where the Rolls stood. He opened the door, tossed her on to the front seat and said curtly: 'Get that wet jacket off—and your shoes.'

Not her shoes, she warned herself silently. She couldn't run away without shoes, and she would have to do that somehow or other; to go back to Crispin's house with him was unthinkable. She fought with the buttons of her jacket with numb fingers while the idea of getting money from him in some way or other crept into her tired head, until the doctor took her hands from the buttons and undid them for her in an impatient manner, then tossed her jacket on to the back seat in very much the same way as he had tossed her on to the front one, then he took off her shoes and reached behind him for a mohair rug, into which he wrapped her with impersonal care before unscrewing a small silver flask.

'Drink this,' he commanded her in a no-nonsense voice, and when she said: 'No, I won't,' went on, still in the same icy rage: 'If you don't, I shall pour it down your throat.'

Araminta opened her mouth then and gulped and spluttered and coughed, and by the time she had her breath Crispin was in the car beside her and the engine was purring gently. The brandy spread its warmth around her insides, creeping into her arms and legs; it also made her feel very peculiar. She made an effort to think clearly, for undoubtedly she would have to have it out with Crispin, and what better time than now? She was wide awake now and not quite as cold as she had been, and she was curious to know just how he had found her. Once they were clear of the town she would ask him to stop and they could each say what they had to say… She essayed to tell him so, gave a small hiccup, and went to sleep.

Her companion made a small sound which might have been a laugh, slowed the car long enough to draw her close so that her head rested against his shoulder, and then sent the Rolls scything its way through a fresh downpour of rain. It was pitch dark now and the curtain of water made it difficult to see, but Crispin didn't slacken speed. They had joined the motorway now, going north to Eindhoven, and there was almost no traffic. Presently the rain became torrential and far ahead of them there was a flicker of lightning. The doctor glanced at the dashboard clock and then at Araminta curled up beside him, dead to the world, and pulled into the next parking bay.

It took a few minutes to waken her and even then she wasn't in full possession of her wits. 'When did you eat last?' he wanted to know.

Araminta opened her eyes unwillingly. 'Breakfast.'

'Supper before that?'

She shook her head, and shook it again when he asked: 'And did you sleep at all last night?' and then feeling that she wasn't being polite, she mumbled 'No,' before her head tumbled sideways against him again.

The doctor started the car once more, driving slowly

now, looking for the signpost he sought. Presently he turned off the motorway into a narrow country lane, awash with water, which led through a small village and then beyond it, curving through fields until it made a final bend into a much larger village with a cobbled street with high walls on either side of it. Its centre was taken up by a church, dimly lighted by a few street lamps, and facing it a row of houses showing a lighted window here and there. Crispin stopped the car and got out into the downpour, to cross the road and inspect the largest of the buildings which bore the appearance of an hotel—which it was, but empty and dark and closed for the winter months. He muttered something under his breath and was about to retrace his steps when he noticed that a few doors down the street there was an inn, its lighted windows revealed it to be small and distinctly cosy, with lace curtains at its windows. Someone inside was playing an accordion and there was a good deal of cheerful noise besides.

The doctor pushed open the door and looked around him, nodding a civil good evening to the half dozen people sitting in the coffee room—a distinctly old-fashioned apartment, its dark panelled walls hung with heavily framed pictures, a huge stove, crowned with an ornate metal cap, jutted out into the room from under an overmantel bristling with old pistols and pewter tankards, and the tables and chairs were arranged with almost military precision around its walls. At the farther end there was a bar, very old-fashioned and massive too, with an enormous mirror behind it, freely ornamented with fretwork shelves and an elaborately carved frame. Crispin took in these antiquated features in one all-embracing glance, he also took lightning stock of the pleasant-faced, elderly woman watching him from behind the bar. Without further hesitation he crossed the room and addressed himself to her.

Araminta woke up again as the doctor lifted her from the car and asked in a panicky voice: 'Where are we? What are you doing?'

Crispin didn't pause on his way over the cobbles back to the inn door, and since it was still teeming with rain, she could hardly have blamed him. He kicked the door open with a foot, set her down at a table nearby and observed: 'We're in the village of Thorn—south of Eindhoven. The weather is too bad to go on; besides, you need a meal and a night's sleep. Sit there while I find somewhere to put the car, and don't let us have any nonsense about running away—you have no shoes and we are both much too tired to splash around in this confounded weather. Drink your coffee when it comes and don't worry about speaking to anyone—I told the landlady that you're English.'

She peered at him, her tired, unmade-up face framed by the soft wool of the rug. 'Are you still angry?' she wanted to know.

He didn't answer her, only smiled a little and went away, and a moment later a young girl came with a tray of coffee. It was hot and creamy and sweet and there were little biscuits in the saucers. Araminta ate hers at once, aware that she was famished, then sipped the coffee slowly, her hungry eyes on the biscuit in the other saucer—presently she ate that one too.

Crispin was taking a long time, she thought uneasily. Supposing he had driven off and left her? The preposterous idea took root in her muddled head and swelled out of all proportions, to disappear like a pricked balloon when he opened the door and came in, sat down opposite her and put her jacket, shoes and bag on the chair between them.

The woman from behind the bar came with fresh coffee and the menu card, and Araminta said apologetically: 'I ate your biscuit…'

The doctor gave her a quick glance and picked up the card. 'Soup?' he asked her, and there was no hint of rage in his face now. '*Echte soup,* I think—there's not much choice, I'm afraid, but there are *gehakt balletjes and pommes frites*. What would you like to drink? I doubt if they serve tea—how about more coffee?'

He gave the order, hung his Burberry on the old-fashioned coat stand by the door and sat down again to sip his coffee, his face still blandly impassive. Araminta, feeling better after the coffee, eyed him doubtfully. Perhaps this wasn't quite the place in which to have a serious discussion, but provided they both kept their tempers… She began in a carefully polite voice: 'How did you know where I was? I thought Valkenburg was a long way away…'

'Not far enough, Araminta.' His eyes glinted beneath their lids. 'I was fortunate enough to find the clerk who sold you your ticket—he remembered you.' He didn't mention how long it had taken him to do that, or how many clerks he had searched out and asked before he had been successful.

'Oh, I should have thought of that—my Dutch…'

'Your pretty face, Araminta,' he corrected her gently.

She decided to ignore that. 'But you didn't know where I was in Valkenburg.'

He shrugged. 'It's not a very large town. The hotel at which you stayed was the third one I visited. They didn't know where you were, but one of the waiters had seen you walking back into the town—it was just a question of looking.'

She said 'Oh,' again, at a loss for words, but presently she said: 'It was very kind of you to come after me, but unnecessary—I'm perfectly all right, you know, and I—I knew exactly what I was doing.'

His stern mouth curved just a little. 'Yes.' He might have added more, but just then the soup arrived and instead of speaking he watched Araminta's delightful nose twitch at its appetising smell. He passed her the salt and enquired in an off-hand manner: 'What did you have instead of supper last night?'

She didn't look at him. 'Well, I—I wasn't hungry. I bought a bag of chips and then I had coffee at the hotel.' She picked up her spoon then and he forbore from asking any more questions, leaving her to enjoy her meal.

The *gehakt balletjes,* richly brown and crisp, tasted like heaven. Araminta ate them slowly and the chips and *appelmoes* besides, thankful that her companion was leaving her in peace. The thought reminded her that even though he might wish to remain silent, there were several things she must say. She accepted yet more coffee and when he offered her brandy to go with it, prudently refused. 'The brandy you gave me to drink,' she reminded him coldly, 'was very strong; it sent me to sleep.'

His eyes gleamed with laughter. 'It does have that effect on an empty stomach, and I neglected to ask you whether yours was empty or not. I'm sorry.' He smiled properly for the first time and she said quickly: 'But you wanted that, didn't you, so that I would go with you without a fuss—how very unfair!'

'Everything's fair in love and war, Araminta.'

She put down her coffee cup, noticing that her hand was shaking. He must be very anxious to be rid of her—Tante Maybella had been right, and nothing was turning out as she had planned. She had meant to disappear without a fuss and write a letter—a dignified letter, betraying none of her feelings—when she got home to Dunster, instead of which she had merely given him a great deal of trouble of leaving him free to go to his Nelissa with a clear conscience. She wondered briefly if Nelissa was a nice girl and said meekly: I'm sorry I've been such a nuisance. Everything went wrong—I should have stopped and packed some things and made sure that I had my notecase with me…but you see I thought that if I could get away before you got home…'

The doctor eyed her narrowly across the table, but she wasn't looking at him. 'I should like to talk…' she began once more.

He interrupted her very firmly. 'And so should I; I fancy we have a great deal to say to each other, Araminta, but not now. You are too tired, and so, for that matter, am I. Tomorrow will be time enough. Now you will go to bed and sleep.'

He got up as he spoke and she got to her feet reluctantly, for she had screwed up her courage and now it was oozing out of her again, but he was right, of course. So bade him good night without another word and followed the young girl up a narrow uncarpeted flight of stairs and into a small, very clean bedroom, where she was made to understand that she was to let her guide have her damp skirt. She supposed that that too was to be cleaned, together with her jacket and shoes, which, Crispin had already told her, would be returned to her in the morning.

He had been as good as his word. Not only were they

returned to her dry and pressed and the shoes shining, but the girl brought her a tray of tea in the morning, as well. True, the tea was in a glass and there was no milk, but it was a nice normal way in which to start the day, although whether the day itself was going to be normal remained to be seen. There was a note under the miniature teapot, too, in Crispin's wellnigh unreadable scrawl: 'I imagine you might not get up without your tea. Breakfast is in half an hour.'

'Orders, orders!' muttered Araminta pettishly, and swept the hair out of her eyes and drank her tea, then got out of her comfortable bed and dressed herself, taking a defiant extra five minutes over her exquisitely neat hair-do. But if she had hoped to annoy the doctor by this, she was disappointed, for he merely put down his paper, got to his feet, wished her an austere good morning and hoped that she had slept well. He then asked her if she would like coffee with her breakfast, sat down again and resumed his reading. There was no one else in the coffee room, so it was an excellent opportunity to state her case, even borrow some money from him so that she might carry out her still nebulous plans to run away again, but somehow it was difficult to address herself to an upheld newspaper.

When their breakfast came, Araminta ate and drank mechanically, rehearsing what she would say when she had the chance, and presently, when he lowered his newspaper, the chance came. Even then, she found it difficult to begin, for he made some matter-of-fact remark about the weather which quite put her off her stroke, although she did finally achieve: 'You said we might talk...'

He was looking over the bill the landlady had just presented, but he put it down so that he might give her his full attention. 'Ah, yes—and so we will, but not, I think, until we have Tante Maybella with us. It would only be a waste of time and we should be at loggerheads.'

'We shan't...I won't come back with you, I won't... can't you see?' Her voice rose a little.

'No, I don't see,' he told her, 'but I believe I can guess...afraid to come back?'

'Of course not—it's simply that there's no point...I don't know why you pretended to...' She stopped, for she was making no headway at all, and Crispin must have shared her view, for he said gravely: 'You know, you haven't finished a single sentence since we started this conversation—I think it would be better if we waited.'

His manner was pleasant, faintly amused now, and wholly impersonal; it was impossible to imagine that this was the same man who had called her his darling, although it wasn't very wise to remember that now.

'If you had told me about her—right at the beginning,' said Araminta wistfully.

His eyes were steady on her face. 'About her?' he queried softly.

'Nelissa.'

He said sharply. 'Ah—Aunt Maybella *has* been talking to you.'

'Yes.'

He didn't say anything for a minute or two but got to his feet. 'We will go home now,' he told her. 'There is a great deal to say to you, but I prefer to wait until we are there. If when we have had our—er—discussion, you still wish to go back to Dunster, you have only to say so and I will arrange for you to go immediately.'

It was a handsome offer and she could see that there was no alternative; he would stop her if she tried to make off, and if he couldn't stop her he would come after her. 'Purely from a sense of duty,' she reminded herself sadly. So she said: 'Very well, I'll get my bag,' in a wooden voice and went back to her little room to fetch it. But when she reached it she sat down on the little bed to think. Things weren't turning out the way she had wanted them to; Crispin was determined to take her back with him; perhaps his sense of hospitality had been outraged and he wished to make amends. He had liked her even if he hadn't loved her; possibly, if Nelissa hadn't suddenly become available, they might have been quite happily married. She sighed; she would have been, anyway.

She got up and went to look at her face in the very small looking-glass which was all the hotel allowed its guests as a concession to their vanity; she looked awful, no wonder Crispin hadn't bothered to look at her during breakfast. She picked up her bag and went downstairs to find the Rolls, polished and gleaming from some hardworking, invisible hand, standing before the inn door. There was no sign of Crispin, and she looked around in a sudden absurd state of panic, quite forgetful of her brave resolve to run away if she had the chance, aware that it was ridiculous to feel utterly lost just because he wasn't there. After all, she was going to have to manage without him for the rest of her life, wasn't she?

She didn't hear him come up behind her. 'I've been listening to the weather report,' he observed mildly. 'More bad weather on the way, I'm afraid, but we should be home in time for lunch.'

He ushered her into the car, talking about the village as he did so—a small feudal town, he told her, owned by one family for a very long time, hence its pristine appearance, its cobbled streets and its air of not belonging to modern times. Araminta listened with half an ear, her mind already kilometres away, in Amsterdam, trying to think what she should do, and say, when they got there. She observed politely that the information was fascinating, and the doctor, who had passed on to some mundane remark about the state of the road, hid a smile as he started the car.

He talked for a good part of their journey, seemingly oblivious of the fact that her replies were distrait to say the least, and when they reached s'Hertogenbosch, he left the motorway briefly and took her to the Chalet Royal for coffee. The leaden sky which had been brooding over them since they had left Thorn dissolved into a torrent of rain while they were drinking it, made worse by the strong wind which came from nowhere to toss the bare branches of the trees and turn hastily opened umbrellas inside out. Araminta gazed out of the window and shuddered despite the luxurious warmth of the restaurant. What would she have done and where would she have gone if Crispin hadn't found her? Something of her feelings must have shown on her face, for he leaned forward to say: 'Don't think about it now, Araminta. Shall we go? It's only another sixty miles.' And at the entrance: 'Wait here while I get the car, there's no need for us both to get wet.'

He was kind, she thought, watching his broad back in its enveloping Burberry weave its way through the other cars to where the Rolls stood. He would be kind to anyone—he could also be, she reminded herself, the nastiest-tempered man she had ever met. Moreover, he liked his own way, he was overbearing too… She saw him get out of the car and walk towards her, unmindful of the rain. A prudent man would have stayed where he was behind the wheel and beckoned… Her heart rocked at the sight of him; he could be as nasty as he chose and marry his Nelissa and forget all about her, but he would be the only man she could ever love. She sloshed through the rain, trying not to notice the grip of his hand on her arm.

The rain turned to sleet as they neared Utrecht and then almost imperceptibly to snow, but the Rolls speeded along the straight ribbon of highway ahead of them, cutting the slowly whitening fields on either side of them in two.

'It's winter,' said Araminta.

'The edge of winter—the first uncertain days of cold and snow and wind. The seasons have their uncertainties as well as us, you know.'

'I'm not in the least uncertain,' she assured him, too quickly.

'Good. Neither am I.' He slowed the car to edge it into the Amsterdam lane and presently they were in the outskirts and then the heart of the city. She had had hours in which to think, thought Araminta, and she had wasted them; she had used her wits to no good purpose and her mind was most regrettably blank. She saw the familiar *grachten,* veiled in snow now and quite beautiful, and in no time at all Crispin was stopping before the house, hurrying her across the pavement and up the steps and in through the door, and there was Jos coming to meet them across the hall. His 'Good morning, doctor, good morning, Miss Shaw' was very correct, although he did allow the faint flicker of a satisfied smile to cross his blunt features.

Araminta gave him a shy smile and stood uncertainly. A ridiculous, vague idea of flight, back through the solid door behind her and into the icy street, had taken possession of her once again. 'I shouldn't,' said the doctor, so that she jumped and went pink. 'I must say you're a very persistent girl. Go upstairs and comb your hair,' he suggested. 'Lunch will be ready.'

She stood her ground. 'You said we could talk…'

He looked shocked. 'My dear girl, on an empty stomach? Unthinkable! Now make haste, do.'

CHAPTER NINE

HER ROOM LOOKED exactly as it had done when she had left it, although when she looked round she saw that the bed had been made up with fresh linen, there were violets and baby cyclamen in the cloisonné bowl on the bedside table and a fresh stock of magazines and English newspapers, and in the bathroom there was a pile of fluffy pink towels and a fresh assortment of soaps, for all the world as though someone had known that she would be returning. Had Crispin been so certain of finding her that he had given orders for her room to be got ready? She took off her jacket and wandered over to the window and stared out. When someone tapped on the door she said 'Come in' without thinking.

It was Crispin. He said at once and gently: 'Now stop mooning about, Araminta. You're on the wrong tack, and the more you puzzle the more wrong you'll get. Come along—you'll feel better when you've had a meal.'

He crossed the room and took her hand, and when she protested that she hadn't tidied herself, said in the same gentle voice: 'Never mind, you look very nice,' and bent to kiss her surprised mouth.

'Oh!' exclaimed Araminta, and went on quite

fiercely: 'Why didn't you tell me about Nelissa?' she paused to swallow tears. 'It was unfair—if I'd known about her and you I'd never have come, and if I'd been told after we got here I'd have gone back home, and now, when I'm trying to put things right, you're making it as difficult as possible.'

Crispin was staring at her, standing very still. He said slowly: 'I wonder just what Tante Maybella told you…'

'Well, it doesn't matter, does it, and if she hadn't, I wouldn't have know…'

'I'm not sure about that. Araminta, Nelissa died sixteen years ago.' He went to the door and held it open. 'Shall we go down?'

Araminta had gone rather pale, but she didn't move an inch. 'I should like to know…' she began just a little shrilly.

'All in good time.' He smiled at her, a smile to turn her heart over and take her breath. 'My darling girl,' he said as she went past him.

They lunched in the little sitting room at the back of the house with the animals for company and Jos to wait on them. He urged Araminta in a low, fatherly voice to try the excellent soup Frone had made especially for her, and when she had obediently supped it up, he begged her to try the turbot, backed up by Crispin's: 'You had better do so, my girl, or you will offend Frone. Jos, I suppose you and she put your heads together over the sweet?'

'Indeed, yes—Miss Shaw's favourite—vacherin.'

'Splendid—will you tell Frone that lunch is delicious?'

After that, Araminta had no option but to accept whatever was put on her plate and eat it, and indeed she had to admit that she felt the better for it, and the wine Crispin had poured for her made her feel better still. All the same, she refused a second glass with a look at him which made him chuckle.

'Keeping a clear head, Araminta?' he wanted to know.

Her head hadn't been clear for some time, not since he had called her his darling girl and told her that Nelissa was dead, but she was given no chance to brood over this, for Crispin kept up a gentle flow of talk which required little or no answer but required her attention at the same, so that although she still felt very muddled and bewildered by the time they went into the drawing room she was much more in command of herself. The coffee tray had already been carried in and Crispin turned back to say something to Jos, who went upstairs.

'Tante Maybella is to join us for coffee,' said Crispin, 'she has already lunched in her room.'

Araminta had sat down, but she got up again as the old lady came into the room. She looked very small and fragile and frightened, even when Crispin had kissed her with his usual kindness and settled her in her usual chair by the fire and invited her to pour the coffee.

'You see that I have brought Araminta back home again,' he remarked cheerfully as he dispensed the coffee cups, and Mevrouw van Sibbelt darted a glance at him, looking more alarmed than ever and most dreadfully unhappy. 'We shall be married quite soon,' he went on, taking no notice at all of Araminta's astounded gasp. 'She will find it wonderful to have you here, teaching her how to run the house and care for its treasures, and I hope to love them, just as you do, my dear.'

'Oh, Crispin, I never meant to… I've been a wicked old woman…you want me to stay? to live here after you are married?' The old, anxious face puckered. 'I thought that if you married, you wouldn't want me…'

Crispin was standing with his back to the fire. 'Is that why you told Araminta about Nelissa, Tante Maybella? Allowing her to think…well, never mind that now, but there was no need. How could you have thought such a thing of me? Home wouldn't be home without you. Isn't that true, Araminta?'

Thus addressed, Araminta made shift to close her mouth which had been hanging open in surprise and then murmur something or other. The nerve, the colossal nerve, taking it for granted that she would accept the situation like a lamb! So she was to marry him now, was she, without a word of explanation? Her bosom heaved with her strong emotions and the doctor's eye lingered lovingly on her. Her own eyes kindled with temper as she prepared to tell him just what she thought of him. Love him with all her heart she might, but he could annoy her more than anyone she knew. Only, on the point of embarking on impassioned speech, her gaze fell upon Mevrouw van Sibbelt and at the sight of that small, unhappy face, her own unhappy ill feelings disappeared entirely. She flew across the room and cast herself down on her knees beside the old lady's chair.

'Of course it's true,' she declared strongly, 'and how could I possibly manage to run a great house like this without you to guide me? I'd be lost, I would indeed.' She put her arms round the thin shoulders and kissed the delicately made-up cheek. 'Oh, you must forget that you ever thought such a thing of us…'

'You're not angry? I am very fond of you, Araminta dear—I don't know what came over me. It was very wrong of me, I have known that, but I'm old, you see, and I was afraid. The old aren't always wanted, you know. And I didn't mean to tell you a lie, exactly, but you made it very easy. I have been very unhappy, for I never thought that you would go away. You're quite sure…'

'Quite, quite sure. Now will you not drink your coffee?'

Tante Maybella accepted the fragile cup and sipped daintily. 'There is a great deal I can teach you, my dear, and so much to tell you about this house, although I suppose Crispin has already told you a great deal.' Her voice faltered a little. 'You are not angry, Crispin?'

'No, my dear.' His voice was very kind, so was his smile. 'How could I be angry with someone to whom I am devoted?'

His aunt put down her cup. 'There, now I am happy again; it is such a relief, and now I think I should like to go to my room and sit quietly. I have a great deal to think about, and the wedding to consider.'

She kissed Araminta and took Crispin's arm. 'You will be very happy, just like your dear father and mother.' She trotted to the door, her arm in his. 'It will be delightful to have children in the house,' she observed happily as he ushered her out of the room.

There was silence after she had gone. Crispin closed the door and leaned against it, his hands in his pockets, and Araminta, aware that he was watching her intently, fidgeted with her coffee cup, then put it down and fell to examining her nails. At last he said: 'I expected a torrent of abuse.'

'Well, I can't think of anything to say.' Whereupon she burst into speech. 'I don't know why you couldn't have told me—you had only to say…at Valkenburg or that funny little inn, and all you could say was that we must wait for your aunt.' Her voice rose a little. 'I can't understand at all. Besides that, you made it very awkward for me, having to tell Mevrouw van Sibbelt…' She added with elaborate casualness: 'Who was Nelissa?'

Crispin was across the room and she found herself wrapped tenderly in his arms. 'That's better,' he spoke on a laugh. 'What would have been the use of telling you anything, my darling love? Would you have believed a word of it? In any case, when I found you you were in no fit state to listen, were you? I should have told you before; I was going to tell you, but the telephone rang and I had to go—remember? And I had no idea why you had run away. I only knew that I had to get you back.' He kissed her swiftly. 'I haven't thought of Nelissa for a long time now. Sixteen years is a long time, my darling, and I haven't thought of anything or anyone but you since I first saw you standing defiantly below those Cornish cliffs.'

'You were very rude,' said Araminta.

'I was thunderstruck—to come across my dream girl in such an unlikely place. I wanted to kiss you…which reminds me…'

This time his kiss wasn't gentle or brief; it was entirely satisfying. Araminta sighed happily. 'I thought—all this time—that you weren't sure about loving me.'

'I've never been more sure of anything in my life, my dearest, but I had to give you time to be sure.'

'I didn't need any time.' She stretched up to kiss him.

'Good—so you won't need any time to think about marrying me. Never mind about clothes and so on, we'll get those later. I arranged about the licence when I was in Dunster.'

She looked at him with loving admiration. 'Since you've gone to so much trouble,' she told him, 'the least I can do is to fall in with your plans.'

* * * * *

Celebrate 60 years of pure reading pleasure with Harlequin®!
Just in time for the holidays,
Silhouette Special Edition® is proud to present
New York Times *bestselling author*
Kathleen Eagle's
ONE COWBOY, ONE CHRISTMAS

Rodeo rider Zach Beaudry was a travelin' man—until he broke down in middle-of-nowhere South Dakota during a deep freeze. That's when an angel came to his rescue….

"Don't die on me. Come on, Zel. You know how much I love you, girl. You're all I've got. Don't do this to me here. Not *now*."

But Zelda had quit on him, and Zach Beaudry had no one to blame but himself. He'd taken his sweet time hitting the road, and then miscalculated a shortcut. For all he knew he was a hundred miles from gas. But even if they were sitting next to a pump, the ten dollars he had in his pocket wouldn't get him out of South Dakota, which was not where he wanted to be right now. Not even his beloved pickup truck, Zelda, could get him much of anywhere on fumes. He was sitting out in the cold in the middle of nowhere. And getting colder.

He shifted the pickup into Neutral and pulled hard on the steering wheel, using the downhill slope to get her off the blacktop and into the roadside grass, where she shuddered to a standstill. He stroked the padded dash. "You'll be safe here."

But Zach would not. It was getting dark, and it was already too damn cold for his cowboy ass. Zach's battered body was a barometer, and he was feeling South Dakota, big time. He'd have given his right arm to be climbing into a hotel hot tub instead of a brutal blast of north wind. The right was his free arm anyway. Damn thing had lost altitude, touched some part of the bull and caused him a scoreless ride last time out.

It wasn't scoring him a ride this night, either. A carload of teenagers whizzed by, topping off the insult by laying on the horn as they passed him. It was at least twenty minutes before another vehicle came along. He stepped out and waved both arms this time, damn near getting himself killed. Whatever happened to *do unto others?* In places like this, decent people didn't leave each other stranded in the cold.

His face was feeling stiff, and he figured he'd better start walking before his toes went numb. He struck out for a distant yard light, the only sign of human habitation in sight. He couldn't tell how distant, but he knew he'd be hurting by the time he got there, and he was counting on some kindly old man to be answering the door. No shame among the lame.

It wasn't like Zach was fresh off the operating table—it had been a few months since his last round of repairs—but he hadn't given himself enough time. He'd lopped a couple of weeks off the near end of the doc's estimated recovery time, rigged up a brace, done some heavy-duty taping and climbed onto another bull. Hung in there for five seconds—four seconds past feeling the pop in his hip and three seconds short of the buzzer.

He could still feel the pain shooting down his leg with every step. Only this time he had to pick the damn thing up, swing it forward and drop it down again on his own.

Pride be damned, he just hoped *somebody* would be answering the door at the end of the road. The light in the front window was a good sign.

The four steps to the covered porch might as well

have been four hundred, and he was looking to climb them with a lead weight chained to his left leg. His eyes were just as screwed up as his hip. Big black spots danced around with tiny red flashers, and he couldn't tell what was real and what wasn't. He stumbled over some shrubbery, steadied himself on the porch railing and peered between vertical slats.

There in the front window stood a spruce tree with a silver star affixed to the top. Zach was pretty sure the red sparks were all in his head, but the white lights twinkling by the hundreds throughout the huge tree, those were real. He wasn't too sure about the woman hanging the shiny balls. Most of her hair was caught up on her head and fastened in a curly clump, but the light captured by the escaped bits crowned her with a golden halo. Her face was a soft shadow, her body a willowy silhouette beneath a long white gown. If this was where the mind ran off to when cold started shutting down the rest of the body, then Zach's final worldly thought was, *This ain't such a bad way to go.*

If she would just turn to the window, he could die looking into the eyes of a Christmas angel.

* * * * *

Could this woman from Zach's past get the lonesome cowboy to come in from the cold...for good?
Look for
ONE COWBOY, ONE CHRISTMAS
by Kathleen Eagle
Available December 2009
from Silhouette Special Edition®